Which one was Bethany Cavell?

Definitely not her, Riley thought, surveying the little bit of a thing with honey-brown curls. Because she was with a little boy, and Riley thought it looked like she was trying desperately to be happy for him. Underneath the smile, she looked tired and anxious.

She was the kind of woman who made a man's protective instincts stir uncomfortably. She looked vulnerable as hell, and as if she would spit like a kitten if anyone suggested it to her. She had paused, and was looking around a little anxiously. He felt an uncomfortable sliver of doubt shadow his confidence that this could not be her.

He silently put in a plea. *Don't be her,* he begged the universe. *Don't let that be Bethany Cavell.*

Of course, the universe didn't hear from him all that often and it was likely tuned in to those who begged favors of it more regularly....

CARA COLTER

Guess Who's Coming for Christmas?

To my wonderful nephew,
Travis Craig,
with love.

Recycling programs
for this product may
not exist in your area.

ISBN-13: 978-0-373-36657-6

GUESS WHO'S COMING FOR CHRISTMAS?

Copyright © 2002 by Cara Colter

www.Harlequin.com

Printed in U.S.A.

Cara Colter lives in British Columbia with her partner, Rob, and eleven horses. She has three grown children and a grandson. She is a recent recipient of an *RT Book Reviews* Career Achievement Award in the Love and Laughter category. Cara loves to hear from readers, and you can contact her or learn more about her through her website, www.cara-colter.com.

DEAR SANTA

How are you? Is everything good at the
North Pole? How are the reindeer and elfs?
I have been very good this year. I am a
big help to my aunt, and she needs a lot of help,
let me tell you. I NEED a daddy for Christmas.

Love, Jamie

P.S. Is the North Pole close to heaven?
Everybody tells me my mom is watching over
me, that she is my special angel,
but I need to know for sure. So if this is true
could I have snow for Christmas?

Prologue

"Mrs. Beckett, could you help me write my letter to Santa Claus?"

The gray-haired kindergarten teacher looked up from her desk, and her heart did the same slow melt that it did every single time she looked at Jamie Cavell.

He was a beautiful child—fine, straight black hair, bold cheekbones, the sweetness of his nature stamped into the roundness of his features. But his huge blue sapphire eyes were solemn and without laughter, and he clutched a small teddy bear, worn nubby from much handling, close to his heart.

Normally she asked children to leave the personal items, like toys and teddy bears, at home, but Mrs. Beckett had been told Jamie rarely set the bear down since his mother had died in a car accident just over a year ago. Buddy Bear, dressed today in a natty sweater, was like a member of the class now.

"Of course I'll help you write your letter," Mrs. Beckett said, and reached into her top desk drawer. She selected the special paper, embossed with reindeers pulling a sled.

Jamie's mouth formed a small O at the sight of the paper, and he sighed with satisfaction. He crept close to her, leaned against her knee and closed his eyes.

Pencil poised, she waited, but he was silent for so long that she thought he needed help. But what advice could she offer to a boy who had lost his whole world?

"A computer game?" she suggested lamely. "You enjoy Oregon Trail here at school. Should I put that down on your list?"

Too late, Mrs. Beckett realized the Cavells might not have a computer at home. His aunt, Jamie's guardian, worked—she stretched her mind back to the last parent teacher interview—as a secretary at a real estate office. A humble position that probably did not allow for home computers.

Jamie opened his eyes and gave her a long look that made her feel terribly inadequate.

"I don't want games," he said firmly. "Or toys.

I don't even want a puppy like Bobby asked for or a pony like Mindy."

Mrs. Beckett thought that would make a very brief letter to Santa. "What do you want, then, dear?"

"A daddy."

"Oh, dear," Mrs. Beckett said. "Jamie, I don't really think that—"

But Jamie had tuned her out. His eyes were closed again, and his brow was furrowed in fierce concentration. He squeezed the little brown teddy bear so tight that its black glass eyes appeared to cross.

"Dear Santa," he dictated, "how are you? Is everything good at the North Pole? How are the reindeers and elfs?"

He thought for a moment, and apparently decided that was good enough for small talk. "I have been very good this year. I am a big help to my aunt, and she needs lots of help, let me tell you. I *need* a daddy for Christmas."

Mrs. Beckett hesitated, then wrote it down. "Do you want to tell Santa why, um, you *need* a father?" she asked uncertainly.

Jamie gave her a look of grave sympathy. "I think *Santa* would know why," he said. He looked at what she had written, pondered it and then sighed. "Could you please sign it Love, Jamie?"

She did. "Anything else?"

"Yes. Could you put P.S.?"

Mrs. Beckett smiled, despite herself. "We haven't even done letter writing yet! How do you know about P.S.?" She hoped this meant he'd decided he wanted Oregon Trail, after all, or one of those cute little robot dogs the children were all so wild for this year.

"Because every day my mom would write me a note before she left for work. My baby-sitter or auntie would read it to me. She would say 'I hope you have a good day, or say hi to Bobby for me, or don't forget we are going to McDonald's after I am done work.' And it always said, 'P.S. I love you.' P.S.," Jamie informed Mrs. Beckett softly, "is the most important part."

Mrs. Beckett obediently wrote P.S. at the end of the letter.

"P.S.," Jamie said. "Is the North Pole close to heaven? Everybody keeps telling me my mom is watching over me, that she is my special angel, but I need to know for sure. So, if it's true, could I have some snow for Christmas?"

Mrs. Beckett looked swiftly out the window to hide the sudden glint in her eyes. Pleasant Valley Elementary School was in Tucson, Arizona. The chances of snow for Christmas were beyond remote. There was an occasional faint dusting of white on the peaks of the Santa Catalina mountains, north of Tucson, but some of those peaks were three thousand feet high. Not exactly a nice little Christmas morning hike.

After she had composed herself she retrieved a lovely envelope that matched the stationery. She wrote Santa Claus, North Pole, on it in careful script. She licked the flap and sealed it.

"Would you like me to mail this for you?" she asked, hoping to protect his poor young aunt from the impossibility of these requests.

"No," he said. "My auntie Mommy will do it."

Jamie sometimes referred to his aunt in this fashion. Apparently it was an endearment that predated the death of his mother.

Still, the affection in his voice when he said it conjured up an image of the woman. Bethany Cavell was young and lovely. Though she did not share her nephew's coloring, Mrs. Beckett saw the same sensitivity and sweetness in Bethany's features that she saw in Jamie's. And now, of course, the same pain. And worry.

"Aunt Beth," Jamie told his teacher earnestly, "has really nice stamps that she got special for Christmas. Santa will like them."

Mrs. Beckett reluctantly gave the letter to him, but as it passed from her hand to his, she felt a sudden and strange awareness.

She was aware of how large her hand seemed, compared to his. And how her hand was covered with wrinkles and age spots, and how his seemed so brand-new, somehow, capable of holding hopes and dreams, still, despite his early encounter with tragedy.

For a moment, when both their hands were on the letter, time seemed to be suspended and the air felt oddly and beautifully drenched in light. Mrs. Beckett had a strange and lovely sensation.

It was a sensation of something of herself going into that letter, the part of her that wanted, after all these years, even though she should know better, to still believe in magic. In miracles.

In Christmas.

Chapter 1

Riley Keenan felt foolish, and he was not a man who enjoyed feeling foolish.

Even in the Calgary International Airport, with its distinctive Western theme, he knew he stood out as the real thing.

Six feet two inches of real cowboy. Rugged. Scarred.

Apart.

People swirled around him, holiday joy in the air. It was December 21, the busiest day at the airport, a parking lot attendant had informed him, as if this was a *happy* event.

Women wore Christmas corsages, and men

struggled with bags and boxes stuffed with brightly wrapped parcels. Little girls were proud and pretty in overly frilly red dresses and leotards, and babies were stuffed into ridiculous green elf suits.

The intercom blared out tinny renditions of carols and every transaction with a skycap or a counter girl ended with Merry Christmas.

Merry Christmas, Merry Christmas, Merry Christmas...

There was no escaping it, so Riley stood like a rock, grim and unyielding, in the middle of this untidy wave of people filled with optimism and good cheer.

But it was not the fact that he didn't fit in that had made Riley Keenan feel foolish. No, he was a man who had no interest in fitting in.

He belonged in the wild, high country of the Rocky Mountain foothills and the Kananaskis country located to the west of Calgary. He belonged to high peaks, and to tall trees, to rushing streams, to rock faces and to the untamed meadows, and he knew it.

He was a hard and lonely man and he belonged in those hard and lonely places where few men went, and fewer stayed. He was used to silence, and his own company. He was used to the sounds of cattle and the companionship of horses.

He felt foolish, not because of who he was. He had long ago accepted who he was. No, he felt foolish because he was standing here, entirely out of his element, doing something entirely against his nature.

He hated the fact he was in this airport, surrounded by people who cared about Christmas. But most of all he hated the fact he was holding up a cardboard sign, roughly lettered, with the names of two people he did not know, and truth to tell, did not particularly want to get to know.

Bethany and Jamie Cavell.

The flight from Tucson via Denver was supposed to be in, finally, after being delayed three times and four hours. They were supposed to have arrived at eleven this morning, and it was now going on three in the afternoon.

"Merry Christmas," a lady said, smiling at him after she had hit him in the shins with her suitcase on rollers.

He glanced at her, and whatever was in that glance she recognized was not about Christmas cheer. She scurried away. She would have scurried away a lot quicker and without the Christmas salutation if she could have read his mind.

He was a man entertaining black thoughts directed at his own mother.

And a sweeter woman had probably never been born. No, Mary Keenan was the quintessential little old lady—white-haired, tiny, bespectacled. She was quiet-spoken and she had a heart of pure gold.

But, sweetness aside, it was his mother's fault he was standing here with the stupid sign, and the next time she asked him to paint her house or rearrange her furniture he was going to disappear onto the range for a good long time.

Mary's sweetness was at the heart of this problem. When some flaky lady had phoned her from Arizona and told his mother about wanting to give her nephew snow for Christmas, his mother should have hung up the phone. No need to be polite. That was the logical way to handle crazy people.

But, oh, no. Not his mother. His mother had offered complete strangers use of *his* hunting cabin for Christmas. Not that he was hunting. And not that he was using it. It was the principle of the thing.

The hunting cabin was for hunters. Riley guided for bear in the spring, deer and elk in the fall. His mother looked after the bookings because he was rarely close to his phone.

The fact of the matter was that a hunting cabin for hunters meant a cabin for *men*. A rough place where cigars were smoked, and whiskey drunk and nobody took off their shoes or complained about mice.

"The cabin is not a place for anyone in search of a postcard Christmas," he'd said, firmly.

"Nonsense," his mother said, equally as firmly. "I would have spent Christmas there myself if I'd thought of it. It's beautiful at the cabin in the winter, the trees dripping with snow, the deer and elk feeding on the meadow, the mountains snowcapped in the distance—"

"The water isn't even running," he'd sputtered. "There is nothing like an outhouse to take the romance out of a cabin in winter."

"I'll look after everything," his mother had said cheerfully, unflinching in the face of his disapproval.

"Be sure and get a seat warmer."

His sarcasm was ignored.

"New curtains, and a little scrub here and there and it will look like something out of a storybook," his mother said dreamily.

A storybook! Hunting cabins were not supposed to look like they came out of storybooks. They were supposed to look like they had been stuck together with whatever was lying around, which pretty well summed up his little refuge in the hills.

"How did some lady from Arizona find out about *my* hunting cabin? No, don't tell me. It must have been the feature *Better Homes and Gardens* did on it, right? 'An Old-Fashioned Christmas Complete with Outdoor Facilities.'"

His mother chose to ignore his sarcasm, again. "One of your hunting buddies is married to a friend of hers who heard she was looking for a cabin. Isn't that the nicest coincidence? She had tried everywhere."

Well, that's what happened when you left finding a place to spend Christmas until only two weeks before the big day.

So, Riley did not think it was the nicest coincidence. That's not what he thought at all. He thought it was a downright nasty coincidence. And the hunting buddy who had sicced Lady Arizona and the Kid on him could put a "former" in front of buddy the next time he was looking for a little hunting holiday in Canada.

"Riley, don't be so hard. That woman was desperate. I could hear it in her voice. I'm sure you would have done the same thing if you had talked to her instead of me."

How could his mother not know him at all?

"I sure as hell wouldn't have done the same thing! Desperate women are to be avoided, not invited into your life. Or your hunting cabin."

"You know what she said?" his mother said softly. "She said she was beginning to think there was no room at the inn."

He snorted at that. "Flaky," he said out loud. But inside he felt the tiniest little shiver of apprehension. Because the cabin was no inn. Many years ago, when he was still a boy, he remembered he and his father working side by side, harvesting the gray timber logs out of the old horse barn his grandfather had built, to make that cabin.

He realized, with grave discomfort, that would

make the building more like a stable than an inn. Now who was being flaky?

Flaky people had a tendency to do that. Eccentricity was a malady that was contagious, a computer virus that invaded the normal thought processes of ordinary people and infected them. The hunting cabin was more like a stable than an inn. Jeez. The Seeker of Snow, whoever she was, was doing it already, infecting his rational mind, and she wasn't here yet. And hopefully never would be.

"I don't want her here," he said, firmly. It was his cabin, after all.

"Have you no Christmas spirit?" He had tried not to flinch, but he had felt every muscle in his body tense under the reprimand. And then his mother had turned, and caught the look on his face before he had time to hide it. "Oh, Riley, I'm sorry. But it's so long ago. Can't you—"

But he couldn't.

"You do what you want," he said to his mother, as if she wouldn't do exactly what she wanted, anyway. "But I'm not having any part of it."

The hunting cabin was located in the hills, in the far southeast corner of his property on a piece of timbered land. It was in the shadow of the Rockies, and bordered Kananaskis, an Alberta Provincial Park. It was in a remote and wild place. The road was barely a road, and on a good day, if it hadn't snowed, it took half an hour to get there from his house. The road was tricky, too. It had soft spots and switchbacks and drop-offs. It was not a road for the faint of heart.

Which his mother had never been. Still, it should have made him feel guilty that his sixty-something mother drove from her own place in town every day, to that cabin, her little four-wheel drive that looked more like a toy than a truck loaded down with clean sheets and new curtains, and all kinds of other stuff that hunters didn't require.

His mother seemed to be having the time of her life fixing up that decrepit little cabin for her mystery Christmas visitors.

He did his best to ignore her enthusiasm, even when she would drop by his place on her way back into town and try to win him over with cookies.

But then the call had come.

"Riley, you won't believe what's happened!" his mother said in that breathless, excited voice that he should have recognized as a harbinger for disaster.

What had happened was that Myrtle Spincher's husband had the gall to up and die just two weeks before he and Myrtle's annual trip to the Bahamas. His mother's friend Alva had come into the tickets.

"Riley, what would you think if I went? I wouldn't be here for Christmas, though. You'd be all alone."

He managed, barely, to refrain from saying

Thank God. It would be a relief to have Christmas to himself.

Then he could ignore it completely.

No cozy Christmas dinner at his mother's place where he had to choke down the turkey, and make small talk with whatever twittering old girls she had rounded up for the festivities this year.

Where he had to smile and unwrap his gifts just as if he was the same man he had been before.

He'd actually encouraged her to go the Bahamas, convinced her, overcome every one of her objections and doubts.

And then, after she'd done everything except pack her bag, she'd reminded him, ever so sweetly, that there was a teeny-tiny complication.

A complication named Cavell arriving from Arizona.

And so while his mother sipped dark rum cocktails on a beach in the Bahamas, Riley stood in the Calgary International Airport for the second time in less than a week, only this time his humiliation was complete.

Because this time he was holding a stupid cardboard sign, feeling foolish and thinking black thoughts toward his own mother.

A new wave of people was coming out through the frosted doors of Canada Customs now, and he scanned them unhappily, mentally eliminating those it wouldn't be.

Nope, not that young family. And not that white-haired couple.

And definitely not her.

She was cute as a button, a little sprite of a thing with loose honey-brown curls protruding from under a red Santa hat. She was nearly hidden behind a cart that held more luggage than most people would need for a year.

Despite the Santa hat, he decided she looked like the woman least likely to do anything impulsive. She had obviously packed everything but a parachute, the kind who thought over every possibility carefully, and who would never hop on an airplane in search of snow.

She was with a little boy, and Riley thought it looked like she was trying desperately to look like she was happy for him. Underneath the smile, she looked tired and anxious.

She was the kind of woman who made a man's protective instincts stir uncomfortably. She looked vulnerable as hell, and like she would spit like a kitten if anyone suggested it to her.

He should be looking for the Cavells, but something about the woman held his attention, even when he ordered himself to look away. He tried to dissect what her pull was.

She was cute but unremarkable. Her clothes, aside from the ludicrous bright-red furry hat, looked like they had been deliberately chosen to downplay

her assets. She was wearing a beige slack suit, the
color of porridge, and the slacks were now wrin-
kled. The outfit made her look like a kid trying to
appear more mature than she was, or a librarian on
winter excursion.

Neither of which warranted a second look.

He shook his head, realizing he was not going
to unravel her mystery in a single glance, shocked
that he had even wanted to.

Maybe he'd spent just a little too long by his
lonesome.

She had paused, and was looking around, a little
desperately. He felt an uncomfortable sliver of doubt
shadow his confidence that this could not be her.

He silently put in a plea. *Don't be her,* he begged
the universe. *Don't let that be Bethany Cavell.*

Of course, the universe didn't hear from him all
that often and it was likely tuned in to those who
begged favors of it more regularly.

He forced himself to look away from the woman.
He searched for anyone else who looked like a Bethany and a Jamie. He had pictured the aunt as being
older, and eccentric, the kid as being cynical and
spoiled.

There was a woman who met that description,
in a fur coat, her nose pointed regally upward. And
she did have a teenager in tow. But she looked im-
periously through his sign when, pride aside, Riley
waved it hopefully in her direction. Another young

woman looked like a possibility but as she drew closer he saw she had two children.

And the redheaded siren with the pudgy freckled boy walking sullenly behind her was now in the arms of a man who was not shy about public displays of affection.

Riley Keenan hated airports.

He hazarded another glance at the librarian in the porridge pants. She looked his way, her eyes wide and anxious, scanning the crowd. And then she saw him. Her eyes locked on his for a moment, and he felt an unwanted zing of energy.

She felt it, too, because she looked swiftly at her feet, flustered, prim. Then she looked back, composed, but her composure lasted less than a breath. She saw the sign.

He fought the temptation to tuck it behind his back and get the hell out of there.

Her eyes lit up with abject dismay, and her gaze moved from the sign to him and back to the sign again.

He knew exactly what she was doing. Begging the universe to change the sign, or him, or both. But he already knew the universe had hauled in its listening shingle for the night.

Apparently six foot two of rugged cowboy was not what the lady had expected. At least he'd already known he was going to be unhappy about who he met at the airport.

Her gaze slid down to her shoes again. She was obviously weighing her options. She sent a glance back toward Customs, but the doors had swung shut behind her, and were labeled clearly No Entry. What did she think she was going to do if she could go back through those doors? Get back on her plane and demand to be returned to Tucson?

Riley waited her out, not quite knowing if he was amused or annoyed by this reaction.

The little boy looked up at her, and tugged on her hand, but that failed to move her toward a decision. So, he began looking around, eyes huge, taking in all the activity and bustle.

The kid had a death grip on a teddy bear. The bear was wearing a red Santa hat, just like the woman's, only it looked slightly less silly on the bear.

And then the boy saw Riley and stared at him with open curiosity. Well, kids liked cowboys. It was part of the joy of being naive.

Then the child saw the sign. He didn't look like he was old enough to read, but obviously he could piece together the letters of his own name.

Riley watched his brow pucker, his lips form around each letter.

And then a light came on in that child's face that was not like anything Riley had ever seen. It was not the kind of reaction he was accustomed to, that was for sure. It was the kind of look a child might reserve for a baseball hero or for Santa Claus.

But for a stranger? A rough cowboy who could think unkind thoughts about his own mother?

There was a certain purity in that boy's gaze. It was downright embarrassing having such adoration bestowed on him when he knew himself to be clearly unworthy of it.

The boy twisted free of the woman's hand and came racing through the crowd, dodging and ducking.

He screeched to a halt in front of Riley and stood staring at him, awe in his face.

"What?" Riley asked, and heard the unfriendliness in his own voice.

"You're him," the boy announced blissfully. And then he wrapped surprisingly strong little arms around Riley's waist, and hugged, hard, oblivious to the fact Riley was wildly trying to disengage him.

"You wouldn't feel that way if you knew what I was thinking about my mother," Riley muttered.

Beth had noticed the cowboy almost as soon as she had emerged from Customs. Who could not notice him? The man stood out from the crowd, big as a mountain, untouched by the surging energy around him.

"Are we in Canada?" Jamie asked, tugging on her hand.

"Yes," she said, looking down at him.

"It doesn't look any different than home," Jamie said, with disappointment.

She was so tired. The flight had been delayed. She had no idea where they were meeting Mrs. Keenan, or how much farther they had to go before they could rest. They had been out of bed at five o'clock this morning and Jamie had dark circles of fatigue under his eyes.

She thought of what this excursion had done to her bank account, and she felt, not for the first time today, foolish. As if she had made a gigantic error, made all kinds of dumb decisions based on emotion instead of coolheaded rationale.

Her gaze was drawn again to the cowboy. Dressed in boots and jeans faded nearly white, a sheepskin-lined jean jacket, a black cowboy hat pulled low over his brow, it struck Beth that the man radiated a raw masculine potency that was both intriguing and threatening.

His face, in the shadow of that hat, was chiseled and hard. His cheekbones were high, his nose had been broken, his features were whisker-roughened, his lips looked stern and unyielding. She was not sure how such ruggedness translated into appeal, but she was aware that it definitely did, and that some part of herself reacted primally to him.

Of course, she was nearly out of her mind with weariness.

His dark gaze was sweeping the crowd, and sud-

denly his eyes were on her. He had caught her staring at him!

And worse, she felt momentarily helpless to look
away from his gaze. He looked so strong and so
decisive.

And so sexy, a voice inside her added.

She blushed, and looked down at her feet. She
reminded the voice, primly, that she was Jamie's
guardian now, and also that she had recently learned
a rather unpleasant lesson about the fickle and self-
centered nature of men. She reminded the voice that
she had made a vow to be chaste and uninvolved
with the opposite sex, which would allow her to be
totally devoted to Jamie until he reached his eigh-
teenth birthday.

For all that, she still glanced back at the cowboy.
And then she saw the sign he carried and it felt like
the bottom was falling out of her world.

This was impossible. She had rented a cabin
from Mrs. Santa, not Mr. Universe. It drove it home
again that she had been stupid and impulsive and
probably made the biggest mistake of her life.

She was in a foreign country! With her young
charge! She was not going off into the unknown
with that man.

Why not? the voice asked her. *Strong and decisive. What you need most right now.*

A man like that, she told the voice firmly, could
make a woman feel like it might be okay to be weak

and vulnerable. What kind of example would that be for Jamie? She had been trying to be a picture of strength for him for over a year now, and some days she even kidded herself into believing she was getting good at it.

She tried to force her tired mind to investigate options. Her eyes skittered to the Customs door. Could she go back through it? Of course she couldn't. But she could get a hotel for the night, book a flight back tomorrow.

Break Jamie's heart and prove she could not be trusted with even such a simple duty as being Santa Claus.

Maybe she should just accept there was no escaping fate, and hers had become tangled from the moment she had opened that letter addressed to Santa Claus at the North Pole.

She'd almost been at the mailbox, when she had stopped in her tracks, the realization hitting her that she was about to mail a letter to a person who did not exist.

And then another realization hit her. *She* was Jamie's Santa Claus now.

Still, she had felt strangely guilty opening that letter, as if she was becoming part of a worldwide conspiracy to trick children. Then she had read the letter, and uncaring of who watched, she sank down onto the curb and read it again.

A daddy?

How could her sweet nephew do this to her, a raw new recruit to the Santa game? Didn't he know he was supposed to ask for a baseball mitt, and a soccer ball, one of those robot dogs the saleslady had assured Beth were the hottest sellers of the season?

Her sister, Penny, and Beth had raised him together right from the start. Not a traditional family, to be sure, but it had still been a family. Jamie had always seemed secure, immensely satisfied with the love of the two women. Penny was Mom. Beth was Auntie Mommy.

The only daddy possibility would have been Beth's boyfriend, Sam, and Jamie hadn't even seemed to like him. Of course, children in general, and Jamie in particular were sensitive to what was authentic and what was not.

And Sam's affection for Beth had been, when put to the test, about as authentic as a three-dollar bill. "It's him or me."

As if she would choose a full-grown man over a child who needed her. As if she would choose a full-grown man who was so self-centered he would ask someone he was supposed to love to make a choice like that!

Beth had looked at the letter again, took a deep breath, forced herself to think. A daddy was out. Absolutely nonnegotiable out. She'd sign Jamie up for Big Brothers since he had made this sudden decision that he was lacking in masculine energy in his life. She felt betrayed. She had tried so hard to be everything, out there pitching baseballs to him, taking him hiking, doing boy things.

The second request was more troubling than the first.

It wasn't just that he wanted snow, he wanted reassurance that Penny was somewhere out there watching him.

It was like Jamie had somehow articulated her own greatest longing. That she be given some sort of sign that her sister, who had always been the strong one, and the decisive one, was somehow there for her still, that she was not bumbling through this all on her own.

But snow as proof of such a thing? Not as impossible a request as it first might seem. It was December. All kinds of places in the world had snow in December. So Tucson, Arizona, wasn't one of them. That problem seemed surmountable, not like the daddy issue at all.

Beth Cavell was not a seeker of adventure. That, too, had been Penny's department. Beth was careful and responsible. Not timid, she told herself, but mature beyond her years.

So it astonished her that it suddenly felt like her life's mission to find snow for Jamie. She didn't have the money for this!

And yet she knew if it took every last dime she had, she was committed to this course.

Snow for Christmas.

And so now, here she stood in a strange city, in a strange airport, looking at a strange man who apparently had her fate in his large, extremely capable looking hands.

Without warning, Jamie twisted free of her grasp, and she watched helplessly as he darted through the crowds. After a stunned moment of hesitation, she pushed her cart through the crowd after him. She realized, thankfully, he had spotted the sign held by the big cowboy, and recognized his name on it.

But her gratitude turned to horror when she saw him wrap his arms around that big man's solid frame and hug him.

Oh, no. Jamie thought Santa had delivered on the daddy!

And how could she set him straight without revealing that she had read his mail?

She became aware of the cowboy's gaze, studying her face. Flinty. Cool. A man who was apparently as pleased about these circumstances as she was.

She would have disliked him, instantly and irrevocably, except for one thing. There was just the faintest edge of panic in those cool, deep-gray eyes, as the big man tried to pry Jamie away from him.

"Mrs. Cavell," he said. His voice was deep and sure. And downright sexy. "I'm Riley Keenan,

Mary's son. She's had to leave the country unex-
pectedly, so I'll take you and your nephew to the
cabin."

In a few short words, how had he made it so plain
that he didn't want her here, and that he resented
being pressed into airport pickup service?

"It's Miss Cavell," she said, and then realized
that place inside her that insisted on noting how
damnably sexy he was had needed desperately for
him to know she was single.

I've sworn off men, she reminded it, *and especially men like him.*

He disengaged Jamie and offered his hand in
one smooth movement. His hand swallowed hers.
His skin was warm and rough, and his grip was
powerful.

And sexy.

It was, Beth told herself firmly, much too early
to decide this trip was going to be a nightmare.

Riley Keenan was methodically unloading her
cart, tucking boxes under his arms, getting a handle on her suitcases.

"Lucky for me you're not staying two weeks,"
he muttered.

"I had to pack my Christmas things," she said defensively, but she was addressing a broad back that
was moving swiftly away from her. Okay, maybe
they were a little closer to the point where she could
declare her Canadian adventure a nightmare.

Jamie took her hand and skipped along beside her singing a happy little song under his breath. Nearly having to run to keep up, they followed the man out the doors of the airport.

It was Jamie who stopped, sniffed the air, scanned the landscape.

"But Auntie Mommy," he said slowly, "there's no snow."

Riley Keenan had stopped and was regarding them impatiently over his shoulder. "Is there a problem?"

"There's no snow," she said desperately.

"We had a Chinook blow in last night. It can melt a pile of snow in a very short time."

"Is there snow at the cabin?" Beth asked, trying not to let it show how close she was to tears.

But she suspected Riley wasn't fooled. He looked closely at her face, and then at the crestfallen child beside her. He scanned the sky, and sniffed the wind.

"We have a saying here—if you don't like the weather, wait five minutes." He shrugged the shoulder strap of one of her bags back into place, and turned again.

He meant there was no snow at the cabin.

She took Jamie's hand and they leaped across a puddle that had been snow just yesterday. She decided she could make it official now. Her Christmas holiday was a nightmare.

Chapter 2

"What a nice truck," Jamie said reverently.

Beth tried to hide her incredulous look, but she noted Riley Keenan did not try to hide his. He lifted a dark slash of an eyebrow. The gesture gave his face a sardonic cast that did not make him less attractive, but rather more intriguing, as if there were dark mysteries in him begging to be explored.

Begging? she reprimanded herself. Penny had always disdained her enjoyment of romance novels, and now here she was face-to-face with a real cowboy, tough, independent, immensely strong, vaguely impatient.

Not a man to be trusted with such a delicate thing

as a child's enthusiasm, she said, and reminded herself, Jamie was her first priority, a priority that precluded exploring male mysteries of any kind.

It was every inch a cowboy's truck, big, old and battered. She thought, underneath the grime, muck and mud, it might be dark blue. She hoped he wouldn't hurt Jamie's feelings by ignoring him, though on the other hand it might help him get over the daddy idea real quick.

"It gets the job done," he said, gruffly to Jamie, sounding completely indifferent, not that Jamie seemed to catch the nuance. He began throwing their luggage into the box with a lack of gentleness that made her wince.

"Those are my Christmas decorations," she ventured, and wished instantly she had been more assertive.

Penny would have said, *Hey! Quit throwing my stuff around, or no tip.*

Tip. She cast the tall cowboy a glance. When he got them to their destination, did she offer him a tip? Not if he broke the Christmas decorations, obviously. Her stomach knotted contemplating this small question. She realized she was completely unsuited to world travel.

"If the baggage handlers couldn't break your stuff, I'm sure I can't, either," he said, but she noticed he was slightly more careful with the next box.

Jamie was busy rubbing mud off the door with

his sleeve, peering at the lettering he'd revealed. "What does this say?" he asked.

Beth squinted at the faded letters. "It says Rocky Ridge Ranch."

"Is that a real ranch?" Jamie asked.

"Yeah." Riley reached over Jamie and around Beth and opened the passenger side door, which she had assumed was locked and wasn't. Though his face was impassive, she detected that he did not enjoy being treated like a valet.

That meant he would scorn a tip, right?

Jamie scampered in and took the middle of the bench seat. Beth climbed in behind him, reluctantly. Her last chance to call it off, to come to her senses. But Riley waited, with elaborate patience, then closed the door with a click behind them, went around and got in his side. He didn't look at either of them. He started the truck.

Out of the corner of her eye, she noticed the jean jacket sleeve slide up as he slammed the truck into gear, revealing the largeness of his forearm, the squareness of his wrist.

"A real ranch with horses?" Jamie asked, providing a pleasant diversion from how appalled Beth was with herself for noticing something so *mundane*.

Utterly masculine, but mundane, just the same.

"Yeah."

A longer answer might have been nicer, since

she was in need of a diversion. She looked out the window, away from his hand on the knob of the gearshift. But instead of taking in the Calgary scenery with the keen interest of a tourist, Beth noticed the cab of the truck smelled good. Of leather and pine, and a tangy, clean smell she couldn't quite put a name to.

Well, maybe she could. Man smell.

"And cows?" Jamie persisted.

"Yeah."

Riley's voice, for all that he didn't seem to like using it, was just as perturbing as that sneak peek at his arm and wrist. Deep. Strong. Sure.

I'm much too tired, Beth told herself as a way of explaining these wayward thoughts. They were skirting the city. Dusk was falling. In the distance, she could see office towers, black against a colorful sky. The road, straight as an arrow, had rolling plains on either side of it, devoid of trees.

And devoid of snow.

They were coming back into the city now, and she noticed brand-new houses, tiny and cozy with neat postage-stamp yards.

The kind of house she would like for Jamie one day, a step up from the mobile home and the park it was in.

"Is Auntie and I's cabin near the horses and cows?"

"No."

"Oh." If Jamie was detecting a certain lack of enthusiasm for his questions, he was undeterred by it. "I've never been in a truck before."

Jamie was apparently determined to get the conversation going.

Riley apparently was just as determined not to. "It can't be that different than riding in a car."

More than one syllable, though she decided it wasn't an improvement. How hard would it be to be nice to a little boy? But again, if he was nice, it would make things too complicated by far.

Beth, with a certain amount of protective instinct, put her arm around Jamie, a gesture she suspected was not missed. "Look," she said enthusiastically, to divert Jamie from trying to have a conversation with a cowboy who was not the least interested in having a conversation with him, "a McDonald's."

Jamie frowned at her and shrugged out from under her arm. "We have that at home."

Riley glanced at her, a frown knitting his brow. "I suppose you're hungry?"

His tone that let her know if she was there was a good chance he was going to call out the firing squad, or draw and quarter her, or execute her in whatever fashion hard-bitten men of the range preferred.

"No, I'm not!" she snapped, "But I will need some groceries."

"My mom told me she laid in some." His tone indicated that was the end of that.

His mom. It was very hard to imagine this man with a mother. Most likely to have been left in a cave and raised by wolves.

How could Riley Keenan have a mother as sweet as the woman Beth had spoken to on the phone?

"Believe me," he continued, which was downright talkative for him, "when my mom says she's laying in the food, that means enough grub for you and the boy and six more like you for a year. She's been baking since you called."

Baking. A complete stranger baking for them? Again, such a lovely gesture seemed so wildly at odds with the man sitting across the truck cab from her, who was too impatient to stop and let her get a few groceries!

Okay. He was big. He was intimidating. He was unfriendly. She just wanted to get to the cabin and leave this part of her vacation that involved Riley Keenan behind her. But she had to stand her ground on matters of importance.

She had never stood up for herself with Sam. Making him happy had always seemed so much more rewarding than pursuing her own happiness, a fact that had made Penny roll her eyes with frustration.

Anyhow, look where being Miss Nicey-Nice had gotten her. It had led Sam to believe—jerk that he was—that she would put his happiness ahead of Jamie's as well.

No, it was time for her to turn over a new leaf in the assertiveness department. She imagined what Penny would say.

"Mr. Keenan, I need groceries." Of course, Penny would have left it there, no explanation and no apology, but Beth could not seem to stop herself from tacking on a helpful explanation. "I need a few things that are familiar. So it feels like home to Jamie. We have our little Christmas traditions."

Riley glanced at her and held her gaze for longer than she considered safe, given the amount of traffic, and the tingle she felt in her spine.

His lips, a straight hard line, said nothing, but his eyes, gray and deep, reminding her of ice forming over a clear mountain pond, said it all: *If you wanted home, you should have stayed home*.

She pulled the Santa hat from her head. Jamie had talked her into buying it while they were laid over at the Denver airport. One for her, one for Buddy Bear. At the time, it had seemed like just the right jaunty touch for a woman who had said yes to an adventure, who was going to such terrific lengths to play Santa Claus.

Now, she realized it might impede her desire to be taken seriously.

"Have you got a problem with Jamie and me staying at your mother's cabin?" she asked sharply, and she thought her sister would have been proud of her tone, her no-nonsense demeanor.

"It's not actually my mother's cabin. It's mine."

Penny, no doubt, would have pointed out that didn't change their contract. Tiredly she thought it made the whole tip issue more complicated. "Do *you* have a problem with us being there?" she asked.

His shoulders lifted and fell under the denim of his jacket. He frowned furiously as he did a quick lane change, checked his rearview mirror. After a long time, he said, "No, ma'am, I guess not."

A lie. She decided she should find it reassuring that he was such a bad liar. She stuffed the Santa hat between her and Jamie. She wanted to slide away from his disapproval and out the door, but she drew a deep breath, and said out loud what she thought her sister would say.

"Welcome to Canada, it's a pleasure to have you," she said.

Riley shot her a dirty look as if she hadn't been properly appreciative of his slim effort not to be completely inhospitable.

"We have to have mini turkey," Jamie told him, sensing the sudden tension in the truck, anxious to smooth it over. "My mom and me and Aunt Beth always have mini turkey for Christmas dinner. Always."

"Mini turkey?" Riley said, and then looked like he instantly regretted his interest.

"Little baby ones," Jamie said. "We get one whole one each. But my mom isn't here this year."

"Where's your mom this year?" Again, Beth sensed a certain reluctance on his part to even show the slightest interest, but now he was trying to hide his displeasure at having to chauffeur them around since he had said he had no objection to them being here, and since she'd called him on his rudeness.

"She's in heaven," Jamie said, matter-of-factly.

For a moment, the cab of the truck was very, very quiet. Beth dared to steal a glance at the cowboy. He was looking straight ahead. A traffic light changed from red to green and he put the truck in gear, moved forward, intently focused on the traffic.

She saw a flicker of something around his eyes, the faintest twitch in the jaw joint below his ear. She thought he would let the moment pass, but he didn't.

When he spoke, Riley's voice was missing that familiar hard edge. "I'm sorry, son. That's rough."

Beth felt Jamie stop breathing beside her. *Son.* She closed her eyes. Oh, boy. If he had tried, Riley could not have found words to make her life more difficult. Jamie wanted a daddy. And she didn't want to know that Riley possessed even one ounce of tenderness.

"It's very rough," Jamie agreed solemnly, yawned and leaned his head on Riley's arm. Beth took this to be a very bad thing, that he was leaning his head on a stranger's arm, when he could have just as easily leaned her way.

A stranger who, in Jamie's mind, might be the daddy he had requested from Santa. A stranger who had probably just cemented that belief by casually using the word son.

Oh, Jamie, can't you tell Riley Keenan is not daddy material?

Riley had not moved away from Jamie's head, but he looked stiffly uncomfortable, and at the first supermarket he pulled in with extreme haste.

Who would have thought it was possible to squeal the tires on a truck? Beth thought wryly.

She got out of the truck. "Come with me, Jamie."

For a moment she thought, in the throes of his new love, he might refuse, but the pull of picking his own "turkey" proved too great.

"We'll be right back," Jamie assured the cowboy.

"Great." The tone was just a little too dry to tell if there was sarcasm in it or not.

"Would you like to look after Buddy Bear while Auntie and I go shopping?" Jamie asked, holding up his bear.

Beth held her breath. Jamie had not parted with the bear since Penny had died. She was not prepared for such a momentous occasion to happen so suddenly. And to not include her.

"Nah," Riley said. "I'm not too good in the bear baby-sitting department."

Jamie looked mightily relieved, tucked the bear under his arm and took Beth's hand. They were almost at the door of the supermarket when she heard the soft "hey" behind her.

She turned. Riley was holding out her purse.

"You forgot this."

She blushed as if her bra strap was showing. She noticed a woman's shopping cart teeter dangerously on a curb because the woman was staring at Riley with open interest.

He did not notice the woman. He leaned close to Beth. "I don't think we have mini turkeys in Canada," he told her quietly, sending a quick glance at Jamie. In that glance she saw the faintest hint of humanity.

The last thing she wanted was even the slightest hint that Riley Keenan might be more than hard edges and rough strength.

"Most people call them Cornish game hens," she confided back.

He took a step back from her, studied her for a moment. And then he smiled. Just the faintest little tickle across his lips. "Oh," he said. "Mini turkey."

She turned from him swiftly, and the same curb that had nearly done in that other woman nearly did her in, too. And for the very same reason. His smile was like a light coming on in darkness, the flicker of hope to a sailor lost on a misty sea.

I am not lost, she told herself, though in fact the

image of a boat lost at sea summed up pretty accurately how she had felt since the death of her sister had thrust her into a world she didn't always feel ready to cope with alone. She and Penny had always been a team. Always. And Penny had always been the one with her hand on the helm.

Beth made herself focus on the aisles of the store, to find comfort in the familiarity. The Canadian supermarket was nearly an exact replica of any she would find in Tucson. And sure enough, they had an open freezer chest full of "mini turkeys."

As he did each year, Jamie studied his choices carefully. Beth tried not to think of the man in the truck. She imagined he would be drumming his fingers impatiently on the steering wheel, not a man accustomed to being kept waiting.

"This one for you," Jamie said, finally. "And this one for me. And this one for he." He placed the three choices in her basket with great authority.

"Jamie, we only need two," she told him gently. "Mr. Keenan won't be joining us for Christmas dinner."

"Why not?" Jamie asked, eyes wide and baffled.

"Because we hardly know him," she said taking out Jamie's choice of the game hen for Riley and returning it firmly to the heap. "He'll have other places to go, Jamie."

"He will?" Jamie sounded crestfallen.

Her secret knowledge of the contents of that letter to Santa ate at her. How to gently dissuade her nephew from his plans for Riley Keenan?

"You and I are a family, now," she said softly. "Just you and I."

He studied her sadly, and then his face brightened, as if he knew a secret that she did not. He picked up the rejected Cornish game hen and put it back in the basket. "Just in case," he said. "Christmas is full of surprises, Auntie."

She stared weakly at the tiny frozen bird, such an unlikely symbol of Christmas hope. "So it is, Jamie. So it is."

They picked up a few more of their favorite things—microwave popcorn, red licorice, chocolate milk—and were ready for their adventure.

The Christmas surprises started, unfortunately, right in front of the truck, when the handle on her plastic bag broke, scattering its contents across the parking lot.

"Here."

She was not sure how he had gotten behind her so silently, but Riley was squatted beside her, helping her pick up groceries. She was blushing again, and when his big shoulder brushed hers, she was thankful for the swiftly gathering darkness.

He paused, and she glanced at him. He was holding her bag of microwave popcorn.

"Uh, you did know there was no electricity at the cabin, didn't you?"

"Of course I did," she lied, snatching the popcorn from him.

He was looking at her closely, and she knew herself to be no better a liar than him.

"Do you want to go get some of the regular stuff?"

She hated it that he was being nice to her, as if dropping her groceries all over the place made her like a little old lady in need of a Boy Scout. Didn't he know he was the world's most unlikely Boy Scout?

No electricity?

"Jamie and I like cooking microwave popcorn the old-fashioned way." And she was sure she was going to find out exactly what that meant since there was no electricity.

Why did she keep lying? Because she didn't want to admit to him how little homework she had done for this trip. She wanted to tell him she was always careful, always prepared, that she drove the people around her crazy with her cautiousness. She could tell he was not the kind of man who would approve of whims, and she desperately wanted to tell him she was not the kind of woman who usually gave in to them.

But then it might seem like she was seeking his approval.

He picked up a game hen, shoved it back in the bag, and then he picked up the other two. One, two, three. She watched his brow furrow as that number registered with him.

He said nothing, scooped up the rest of her things, folded them back into the damaged bag and then put it all in the back of the truck.

"Jamie's a big eater," she lied again.

He shrugged. "Ready?" he said.

Another opportunity to get out of this. To tell him to pull over at the nearest hotel. No electricity? How could they have Christmas with no electricity?

But her pride wouldn't allow her to back out. She climbed back in the truck, set her chin proudly, put her Santa hat back on, and said, "Ready."

Three mini turkeys. Unless his mother had forgotten to tell him something, or unless Jamie was really a big eater, three mini turkeys spelled trouble.

Plus, Riley had the bad feeling Beth hadn't known the cabin had no electricity. It was just the type of detail his mother might have a tendency to overlook while she was waxing poetic about the deer and the elk in the snow-covered meadow.

The lack of electricity wasn't a really big deal, not like the lack of indoor plumbing in certain seasons. There was a beautiful, black wood-burning heater at the center of the main room. And the appliances and lights ran off propane. But sliding a glance at her, he realized what was not a big deal to him, might be a bigger deal to her.

There was the kid resting his head against his arm again, glancing constantly at him with shy, adoring looks. There was a little puddle of warmth growing on the arm of his jacket.

Traffic thickened as he headed up Crowchild Trail, and he concentrated hard on that trying to erase *three* mini turkeys from his head.

Well, if they invited him for dinner, he'd just say no. That was easy, wasn't it? He'd signed on to pick them up from the airport, and dump them at the cabin. Anything after that would have to be considered above and beyond the call of duty. Stopping at the grocery store was already more than he'd signed on for.

Traffic eased as he hit the far southwestern outskirts of town and took the Bragg Creek turnoff. He shot Beth a glance from under his lashes and felt his chest heave with relief.

In the soft glow of the dashboard lights, she looked like the woman least likely to invite a strange man to Christmas dinner, even if she was wearing the Santa hat again. Her features were remote. Closed.

The kid, he realized, was a different story. He looked down in the dim glow of the dashboard lights. The child had been so quiet, Riley had thought he might be sleeping. But no, there he was, those huge eyes fastened on Riley as if it was Superman driving the truck.

"What?" he said, a trifle defensively.

"What are those marks on your neck?" Jamie asked softly.

Riley reached up and pulled up his shirt collar, and then his jacket collar. The question he least liked to answer.

"They're burns," he said shortly.

"Jamie," the aunt said, "it's not polite to ask people about things like that."

Riley sent her a black look. Had she seen the scars, then? Was she revolted by them? What the hell did he care?

He was dropping her, the little guy and the mini turkeys off at the cabin, and he wasn't seeing them again until it was time to make this return trip to the airport.

"Where did you get burns from?" Jamie asked.

"Jamie!" his aunt said, mortified.

Personally Riley preferred honest curiosity to surreptitious looks, which unless he was mistaken she was now giving him. She wouldn't be able to see anything in this light. Not that he cared.

"I got burned in a fire," he said.

"Oh," Jamie breathed. "A fireman!"

He decided to let Jamie think what he wanted, but realized there was enough worship in the lad's eyes already. Despite what a whole district wanted to believe, he was no hero. "No, not a fireman. Just somebody who was in the wrong place at the wrong time."

"Do they hurt?"

"No, not anymore."

"But they did once?"

"Jamie, please—"

"They did once. They haven't hurt for a long time." He felt something on his neck, and stiffened.

"Buddy Bear will kiss them better," Jamie told him solemnly.

Riley resisted the impulse to knock Buddy Bear into next week. Instead he suffered the bear's woolly nose against his neck, while Jamie made corresponding kissing noises. He was glad it was dark in the cab, because if he was not mistaken his face was getting red. He was not accustomed to this.

Affection.

After a while the bear's ministrations came to a blessed end, the weight on his arm increased, and he felt the rise and fall of the boy's breath become deep and steady.

"I'm sorry," Beth said. "He doesn't know any better."

"It's okay." He slowed as they passed through the tiny hamlet of Bragg Creek. The silence grew in the truck. He glanced over to see that she was sleeping, too, her eyelashes thick and tangled, her mouth partly opened, her head at an angle that was going to give her a sore neck.

She looked very beautiful sleeping. Like an angel. Innocent.

He felt like he had a truckload full of innocence. And affection. Neither were traits he had been on speaking terms with for a long, long time.

She sputtered awake when he slowed down for his driveway.

"Are we there?" she asked sleepily.

"No. Just passing my place. The cabin's another half hour beyond it."

His house and barn were illuminated by a yard light.

"What a beautiful home," she murmured, and he heard the surprise in her voice. She had expected he would live in a tumble-down shack, which truth to tell would have suited him fine.

Besides she was mistaken about it being a home. She probably lived in a home. Homes had pretty curtains and worn furniture, toys on the floor, and the smell of cookies baking.

This was just a house. Once, he had thought it would be those other things. When he had built it, he had still had such thoughts in his mind.

That his children would fill the bedrooms and play in front of the fireplace.

A dream gone up in smoke, literally.

It's just not fun anymore, Alicia had said, but she had been looking right at those scars. They'd been fresher then, red and angry looking. She had never been able to keep the revulsion out of her beautiful face.

"Do you live there alone?" Beth asked.

"Yeah."

"But it's so big."

He shrugged a none-of-your-business kind of shrug and she got the message. Because of the recent Chinook the track to the cabin had gotten very muddy, and he put the truck in four-wheel. It began to growl its way up hills and through valleys.

It slid once or twice, not too bad, but she gasped as if they were going off a cliff.

Finally they pulled into the clearing, and the cabin sat in his headlights. It was a humble building, just a little box made out of old gray logs. Still, the night lent it some magic. The stars twinkled in an inky sky, the mountains were heavy black in the background. It sat on the edge of a forest, and the huge trees were silent and serene.

"Look," she said, awestruck, as two deer bounded across the meadow that was at the front of the cabin, their tails flagging frantically.

"White-tailed deer," he offered generously since his time as the tour guide was drawing to a close.

He turned off the engine of the truck but left the headlights on. He snagged a few of her boxes out of the back of the truck and went up to the cabin door.

An evergreen bough, decorated with a huge red ribbon bow graced the door.

He shoved it open and went in, swallowed by darkness and cold. He heard her come in behind him, and stop.

"Hang on," he said. He struck a match, and found the light over the kitchen table, turned on the propane. It hissed to life as he held the match up under the mantel.

The light didn't come on all at once like electric light. It glowed slowly and softly to life, and revealed a most amazing transformation.

His rough hunting cabin had been turned into an enchantment.

He looked around with dumbfounded amazement. Red curtains, held back with white ties hung at the windows. Crocheted snowflakes danced in the windowpanes. There was a thick red rug underneath the kitchen table. The rough surface of the table had been covered with a bright tablecloth, red, with white snowflakes decorating the border.

"Oh," she said softly. "It's like a dream."

He glanced over his shoulder at her. Her hands were pressed to her cheeks, her eyes were wide and bright. His mother would have loved this moment—when both he and Beth's surprise was so complete.

Beth's delighted, his a little less so.

How much had his mother spent on this? Probably a whole lot more than she had rented out the cabin for.

He went into the living room, divided from the

kitchen by the potbellied stove, and lit the second lamp.

More red curtains. More Christmas hoopla. Even when it was switched back to a plain old hunting cabin, he had the awful feeling that he was going to be stuck with this much merrier picture burned into the hard drive of his brain.

Out of the corner of his eye, he saw Beth wandering around the room, touching things with awed disbelief.

His mother's best Christmas decorations were all here. Her manger with the three wise men and the camels and donkeys, her Royal Doulton Christmas figurines. Her garlands of fake holly were bordering the ceiling.

"No wonder she went to the Bahamas," he muttered. "She had nothing left."

"Pardon?"

He just glared at her, as if it were her fault a perfectly good hunting cabin had been turned into this. He moved past her and went back outside. He was five minutes from discharging his obligation.

He scooped the rest of the luggage out of the box, saw she had come behind him.

As he came back out of the cabin, very nearly a free man, she was struggling down the walk with the soundly sleeping Jamie in her arms.

Say good-night, he ordered himself, *you can even wish her a Merry Christmas. But go.* But of course he couldn't leave her staggering under the weight of the kid. She was just a wee bit of a thing.

He reached for Jamie.

"I can manage," she said, proud and stubborn.

But he saw, suddenly and clearly, that she couldn't. And it wasn't just Jamie. He was going to have to show her how to light the propane lamps, and the other propane powered fixtures. He was willing to bet she wouldn't even know how to get the fire started.

Sighing, he took the child from her arms, and felt a pain, like the ripping open of a wound. This was a glimpse of the life he was not going to have, now, ever. This would never be his sleeping child being carried in, his life did not hold the subtle, sweet pleasure of looking into a woman's clear eyes under a starry night.

A swift escape from this traitorous feeling inside of himself was mandatory.

He turned on his heel, brought the boy into the cabin, laid him gently on the sofa. It was cold in here, and after hesitating just a moment, he took off his jacket and covered Jamie with it. Jamie's lips moved and he snuggled deep under the cover, but his eyes didn't open.

"So," he said hopefully, "you know how to light a fire, right? And how to use propane fixtures?"

At the look on her face, hope died. Escape was postponed.

Chapter 3

"Paper. Kindling. Match."

The crumpled newspaper burst into flame inside the cast iron stove, and Riley blew gently on the kindling once the paper had burned out, nursing the tiny flame.

"Not too much," he said, feeling foolishly like a Boy Scout leader, "Or you'll blow it back out." Lighting a fire had always struck him as a dance of delicacy and balance not unlike the relationship between a man and a woman. Too much of any one element introduced too soon could put it out. Going too fast could suffocate it.

He did not like it one little bit that he was having

thoughts about the dance between men and women with Bethany Cavell standing beside him, her arms wrapped around herself and her teeth chattering.

A woman meant to be gathered in a man's arms if ever there was one. She had the most intriguing color of eyes he had ever seen. They were green, but they were like emeralds that had been melted and shot through with silver. The effect was smoky and unconsciously sensuous. He caught himself trying to catch another glimpse of them.

Annoyed with himself, he sat back on his heels, and looked deliberately away from her. "Here, you try it. I'm not going to be around to help you with stuff like this."

No, sir, he was a man with a strongly developed sense of self-preservation and when you started thinking a fire was giving you messages about relationships, and you kept trying to sneak peeks at her eyes, trying to find just the right word to describe them, then it was time to exit, and fast.

Bethany got on her knees in front of the stove, tucked her hair behind her ear and blew gently on the flame. This was actually worse than when she'd been watching him. Now, she was too close. He noticed the curve of her shoulder, and the swell of her breast. And when she blew again, he noticed that when a woman shaped her lips like that, it was the very same as if she was getting ready to be kissed.

Okay, the truth was he had never felt less like

a Boy Scout leader. And he'd had about enough of feeling foolish for one night.

He wanted to go home, pull the pillow over his head and forget the scent of her, drifting to him beyond the smell of the wood and the flames licking at it.

She smelled of lemons.

Nothing the slightest bit sexy about lemons, as far as he knew. In fact, his mother had gone through a lemon frenzy recently, claiming the curative powers of citrus. For weeks she had dropped off lemon cookies and lemon muffins and lemon cake and lemon teas until he was so sick of lemon that he would have liked to have it added to a toxic substance list.

But here he was, kneeling next to Beth Cavell on the rough cabin floor, and finding that lemon scent intoxicating, wanting to lean closer, inhale deeper, wanting more. It was enough to make a man lose his head.

That, and the way her hair fell forward, how it looked with the light of the fire highlighting it, turning it from plain old brown to golden, alive with shimmering lights.

"Okay, that's going pretty good," he said when he could no longer stand the heat, and not the heat from the fire, either. "Now we can add something bigger."

In his sudden anxious desperation to get out of

here, he chose a log far too big, and suffocated the fledgling fire as surely as pouring water on it.

He cursed, out loud.

"Let me try it this time," she suggested.

"Have you ever started a fire before?" he asked, not kindly. It was obvious she was a city slicker who would know nothing about fires.

She looked resentful of her competence being questioned. "I've been camping a few times. When I was a kid. I think we had a fire."

Her brow furrowed, with precision and patience, she rebuilt the fire, adding pieces of ever increasing size until it was a Boy Scout perfect fire. Her teeth stopped chattering. The room began to glow with a warmth that matched all the hokey and festive decorations.

She turned to him and smiled. If her smile had been smug, it would have been easy to dislike her intensely. But it wasn't. Her smile revealed small, straight white teeth, and it made her eyes dance.

"Amazing," she said, wiping her hands on her trousers and standing up. "I feel as if I scored the winning run at the final game in the World Series."

"Against the defending champ," he muttered, and stood, too. After all, he'd been building fires all his life. It was as much second nature to him as putting a saddle on a horse.

But on the other hand, if you were going to compare fires to relationships, women were just better at it. More intuitive, more patient, more aware that you couldn't just leap from A to Z ignoring the other letters in the middle.

"That was fun," she said.

Fun. The thing he'd failed at. *You're just not fun anymore,* Alicia had told him. Not that he and Alicia had ever found fun in something so simple as lighting a fire. No, fun had meant wild things to them-driving too fast, partying all night, chasing rodeos, unleashing passion.

Riley realized he did not like how his visitor was triggering memories in him—thoughts of relationships, thoughts of things long past, hurts he had packed away in some mental crate that he had vowed never to reopen.

He was not an introspective man. He was a man of action, and so he sought refuge in action now.

Beth was still smiling like a delighted child. It had taken a ring the size of a marble to make Alicia smile like that.

"It gets warm so fast," Bethany said.

You're not kidding. A man could be heated up and out of his head before he even knew what had hit him.

"Let me show you how to work the lights and the stove, and then I'll go." With her standing much too close, he showed her how to work the stove first, and then the propane lights. He watched closely while she lit them herself. He was aiming for detachment, just assuring himself she could work everything safely. But she had to stretch way up to reach the light.

Nice figure under the librarian outfit. If he was not mistaken, he was actually starting to sweat. The miracles of wood heat and hormones.

There, she had it. The lantern glowed to life and he was treated to another smile. He was out of here.

"Anything else?" he asked out of politeness only, already heading for the door.

"No, I can't think of anything. Oh, except the phone. I don't see it."

"The phone?"

"Where's the phone? You know, in case we have an emergency."

He scowled at her. An emergency? He hadn't even thought of emergencies. He could tell this was going to wreck havoc on his clean getaway.

"There is no phone here," he said.

"What about a cell phone?" she asked, her eyes very wide.

"No service. Too close to that mountain. People kind of come here to get away from it all." Actually, *people* did not come here. Men did. And men never gave one single thought to all that could go wrong.

"But what do I do in case of emergency?" she asked, serious, as if disaster was waiting outside the door to nab her.

"What kind of emergency?" he said, folding his

arms over his chest. It felt like he was looking way down at her.

"What if I broke my leg? Or what if Jamie split his head open?"

Now trust a woman to think of that *after* she was happily ensconced in her wilderness cabin.

"Look," he said with as much patience as he could muster, "I've been falling off rank horses and bad bulls most of my life. I've yet to break a bone or split my head open. What are you and the kid planning on doing up here?"

"I guess if it doesn't snow, we're going to play board games."

Again it seemed to him she might be able to teach him a thing or two about having fun. If he was interested. Which he most definitely wasn't.

"I don't think board games have a danger rating on the workers' comp scale," he said flatly.

She looked hurt that he was making fun of her, and he actually felt a small niggle of guilt. *Don't offer,* he ordered himself. People who put themselves in the path of heat got burned, a life lesson he should know better than just about anybody.

Still, there was his voice. "Do you want me to look in on you from time to time?"

"Oh, no, of course not."

He looked at her narrowly. The confidence was superficial. If he went right below the surface, he would find something else. So, of course, he wasn't going to go looking.

"Good. See you."

"It would be quite a bit of trouble for you to check on us. Wouldn't it?"

Way too much trouble. "I could check in on you."

"No. Never mind. We'll be just fine." She laughed self-consciously. "It's just I've never in my life not been near a phone. And neighbors."

"Isn't that what you wanted when you came here?"

"Actually, what I wanted was snow."

She was scared. He'd worked around enough green horses to be able to just about smell fear. He could tell how hard she was trying not to show it, but he could see it in her eyes, and in the sudden way she was hugging herself as if the cabin was freezing again.

"I'll drop by," he said, and heard the weary resignation in his own voice.

She must have heard it, too. "No! It's okay, really. I'm sure we'll be fine."

But just under the resignation he *felt* something within himself at odds with it. A desire to come back here? A small thing, way at the back of his brain, that had to be stamped out immediately and ruthlessly, like an unwanted spark on a wood floor.

"Great," he said, "have it your way. We'll see you

in a week. On December 28. You'll be back with phones and neighbors by the New Year."

"Fine," she said, much too brightly. "See you then."

He brushed by her.

"You're forgetting your jacket." she said.

He glared at her. Had she figured out his temperature was about one hundred and three? He figured he was the man least in need of a jacket at the moment, but there was no sense letting her see that. She might reach the entirely correct solution that she had something to do with his heated state.

He retrieved his jacket from the sleeping child, remembered her staggering under Jamie's weight and hesitated. "Do you want me to put him to bed?"

"I'll look after it."

See? He was getting out of here just in time. A part of him really wouldn't have minded feeling the almost liquid weight of the child in his arms again.

He yanked on his jacket and opened the door. "Good night," he said.

"Wait." She was reaching for her purse. For one horrible moment he actually thought she was going to try to give him a tip. He gave her a look that she interpreted correctly, because she hooked the purse over her shoulder and let it fall to her side. "If I had to walk out of here, how long would it take me?"

"Sorry?" Riley scrutinized her. He had really thought this subject was closed. Hopefully she was just looking for something to say to cover that awkward moment.

"Like if a bear attacked us or something." She was still on the subject of highly improbable emergencies. Women did that. Made you think they'd left a topic behind, when they really hadn't.

His mother had done that with the cabin. *I'll look after everything.*

Oh, sure. She was probably chatting up some aging millionaire as her favorite son—okay, her only son—was coping with her Christmas fiasco. Was there the teeniest possibility his mother had planned this?

"Bears sleep in the winter," he said, just as if he believed this was really about bears, when he knew it wasn't. It wasn't about her nearly offering him a tip, either.

It was about something much more complicated.

It was about a big, strong man wanting to protect a woman who seemed frail and frightened and out of her league. He was pretty sure Bethany would knock him up the side of the head if he had the nerve to articulate it. Especially because it was true.

"Oh!" She laughed nervously. "I knew that. They hibernate, right?"

"You could walk out of here in half a day, easy," he said by way of reassurance, and eased one foot out the door.

"Half a day!" she exclaimed.

"Or less, depending how fast you walk."

"With a broken leg," she said, trying to be funny and confident, and missing the mark because her eyes were huge and full of anxiety.

A gentleman would offer to stay. No. A gentleman would not offer to stay with a single woman for the night.

What would a gentleman do? Offer his own house? With a phone and electricity and indoor plumbing?

No Christmas decorations, of course.

And come to think of it, he was no gentleman.

"Good night," he said again, tipping his cowboy hat, turning away. He almost succeeded in getting his other foot out the door.

"Does anybody ever come up here?" she asked casually, as if it was just a little something she was curious about. Her voice had a funny little tremble in it.

"Sorry?" He took a tentative step out onto the step, felt the cold air rush over his heated body, looked longingly at his truck.

"Does anybody come up here? Kids looking for parties? Lost hunters?"

"It's not hunting season. You'd have to be pretty desperate for a party to come up here looking." He sighed. "Do you really mean mass murderers? Rapists? Thugs on the run from the law?"

"Of course not," she said haughtily, but she caught her lip between her teeth.

He considered telling her that he'd heard terrorists were looking for caves in this vicinity, but the remark died at the look on her face. "No. No one ever comes up here. Not at this time of year. Never," he said firmly. "You can't get up here without taking the road right past my house. Not that anyone has ever tried. You're safe here, Bethany. Probably safer than you are in your own bed at home."

He was uneasily aware that he liked how her name sounded on his tongue, full and rich, like the first sip of coffee in the morning.

"I know that," she said, and sounded like she was trying to convince herself.

"All right. Good night, then."

"Merry Christmas," she said bravely.

"Yeah. Merry Christmas. Whatever."

He finally made it all the way out the door, a victory that was diminished somewhat by the sound of her clicking the lock on the door behind him. He had really had no idea that door had a lock on it, until just this minute.

He stood on the front step for a minute, savoring the silence, the stars, the clean bite of the cold air. How could anyone be afraid out here?

He was not responsible for the fact she was afraid. There was nothing he could do about it. His obligation to her was over.

He got in his truck and drove down the mountain, but try as he might, he could not help but wonder if she was frightened at this moment. Would she know it was the lonesome songs of the coyotes piercing the cold night air? Would she know that the wind in the trees could make them creak, like an old door on a rusty hinge? Did she know the hoot of an owl, the strident bugle of an elk, the pop of the ice on the pond?

Even in his own bed, finally, he could not sleep, thinking of her questions, of the sound of the door locking behind him. The scent of lemons seemed to be tickling his nostrils and he could see her smoky-green eyes as if she was standing in front of him.

So, he'd run up and check on them in the morning. It would be the gentlemanly thing to do. Nothing wrong with learning to be a gentleman after all these years.

He would consider it his Christmas gift to his mother.

On the other side of the locked door, Beth listened to the truck leave. She pressed her ear against the door until she could hear it no more.

He was gone.

She and Jamie were absolutely on their own.

"Just like the Wilderness Family," she said out loud, as if the sound of her own voice would in some way be reassuring. It wasn't.

"Beth," she told herself firmly, "you have it from a reliable source. There is absolutely nothing to be afraid of."

Having said that, she rechecked the door. It was one of those with a flimsy lock on the handle. A good kick would destroy it. Come to think of it, an intruder wouldn't even need to use the door. He could break the windows. No one to hear the shattering glass, or her screams.

"Beth, way too many episodes of *America's Most Wanted*," she told herself. Still, she went over to the window over the sink, and pressed her nose against it, scanning the inky darkness. A log popped inside the wood heater, and she jumped.

Annoyed with herself, she put away her groceries, did a delighted inventory of the contents of the fridge. She noticed there was a cookie jar full of homemade chocolate chip cookies, and a bread box with fresh bread in it.

The fire cracked, and she jumped again.

"Damn," she said. The truth was she had never been alone. Not like this. No phone. No neighbors. Until a few months ago, she and Penny had always shared accommodations. Silly that that would make her feel safe, but it had. Of course, Penny had not been afraid of anything.

She realized she had not asked enough questions about the cabin. She had been so grateful to find it. Somehow she had assumed it would have electricity, and that it would be close to other cabins. She had imagined a little resort setting, where there would be lots of things to do.

Snow things.

Now that there was no snow, what *were* she and Jamie going to do? Sit here and play board games all by themselves? She had seen the look on Riley's face when she had said that's what they were going to do.

Boring. His expression had condemned them as boring. She didn't even know him. Why did she care what he thought?

She cared.

Despite the cheery decor in the cabin, Bethany wondered, uneasily, if she had set up the most depressing Christmas in history.

Should she have invited Riley for Christmas? It would have made Jamie so happy. But then, of course, she would have had to deal with the inevitable disappointment after, when they were heading back home, sans Daddy.

Who was she kidding that it would have just been for Jamie if she had invited him?

She thought of the scars she had glimpsed on his neck as he crouched beside her to light the fire. Jamie had mentioned them in the truck, but it had been too dark to see them. In the light of the fire she had seen them, though.

They ran along his neck, from his ear to his jaw,

the whole underside of his chin, and then dipped down the column of his neck inside his shirt.

On any other man, she thought the scars might have been unsightly. But on Riley it was different. As if they were a part of him in a way she didn't quite understand. A part of the strength and resiliency and mystery that pulsated out from him like an electrical current.

"You're not going to see him again until it's time to go home," she told herself. "And that's a good thing. A man like that makes life seem confusing and complicated."

A man like that made a woman ask herself questions that were better not asked. What would his lips feel like on hers? What would the texture of his skin be under her fingertips? What would his gray eyes look like if the hard light in them softened?

Holding that happy thought, she explored the far reaches of the cabin, which were not very far reaching. It had this main room, and two tiny bedrooms. No bathroom, the one thing Mrs. Cavell had warned her about.

In the safety of her Tucson trailer, no bathroom had seemed a very minor thing, a part of the great adventure.

Now, the thought that she was going to have to venture outside before she went to bed did nothing to lighten her mood.

She put off the moment as long as she could. She

moved Jamie into the smaller bedroom, kissed his forehead, stroked his hair and looked lovingly at the innocence of his features.

Finally, taking the flashlight from beside the door, she unlocked it. She opened it a crack and looked out furtively. Not a single sound, a somnolent quiet over the landscape that was unsettling. No quiet hum of engines, and tires on pavement. No sound of the neighbor's radio, the odd distant siren, horns honking, teenagers laughing as they made their way home from the local movie theater.

She felt as if she had accidentally landed on the moon, the silence was so unfamiliar and so unnerving.

She took a deep breath and stepped out onto the tiny porch, shutting the cabin door behind her. For a moment it seemed impossibly black, but she didn't turn on the flashlight right away.

She allowed herself to feel the cold. It was like nothing she had ever felt, like little tiny needles tattooing her skin. The air coming in her nose felt like it moved into her lungs with freezing force.

Still, she did not move away from the cold, but stood on the step and allowed her eyes to adjust to the darkness. The stars winked over her, the trees looked like huge, silent guardians.

Suddenly she wanted to know, just as desperately as Jamie did, that she was not all alone. She felt like she needed to be reassured that even though she had done something uncharacteristically stupid and impulsive, that she would be looked after, somehow.

"Penny," she whispered, "are you out there, somewhere? Are you watching us? How could you do this to me? I'm not qualified to be a parent. I'm making a mess out of Santa Claus. I'm going to spoil Jamie's Christmas. I don't have your confidence, your take-charge attitude. I wish I did. Some days I don't know what to do without it. Some days, I can't even make simple decisions, like what to cook for dinner. And then when I have to make a big decision, like coming here, I just jumped in, without looking back. You know that's not like me."

She felt a clog of emotion in her throat, and tried to swallow it back.

"Penny, he just needs to know you're watching out for him. And I need to know, too. That you're looking out for us."

The most amazing thing happened. The sky began to dance. At first it was just the smallest flicker of light, so small she thought she had imagined it. And then it flickered again, as though the sky was a black blanket and light was trying to flutter through from the other side.

Suddenly a plume of iridescent green leaped, trailing color behind it, falling in an arc, like Fourth of July fireworks. The green paled, then leaped again, intense, astonishing. The band of light lengthened and swirled, shimmering with an astonishing array of colors from turquoise to red to green again.

Beth stared, awestruck. She did not know what she was seeing, only that it felt like a miracle. And an answer.

A long time after the last of the lights had flickered out, she became aware she was now very cold. She turned on the flashlight and made her way to the outhouse.

It was a tidy, tiny building, with a half moon cut in the door, just like they had in Western movies.

It was cold!

Moments later, she ran back along the worn path to the cabin. She paused on the porch, but the light show was over. Still, the feeling it had given her remained. A feeling that all would be right with her world. She entered the sheltering warmth of the cabin, and felt a deep and primal sense of gratitude for the cozy little fire burning. She opened the door to the woodstove and put on another log, and then she went to her bedroom.

It wasn't until after she'd put on her pajamas that she wondered if she had locked the door. And then she laughed out loud, free from fear, slipped between sheets that smelled wonderfully clean. The blankets were heavy on top of her. She closed her eyes and slept instantly and deeply.

"Auntie Mommy, it's freezing in here."

She opened her eyes. Jamie was standing beside

her bed, shivering, clutching Buddy Bear as if his life depended on it. Beth could feel the cold in the room on her nose and cheeks. The first morning light was washing in the windows, gray and cold.

She opened up her covers and he slipped into the bed beside her, and she pulled the covers up over their heads to escape the cold. Buddy Bear kissed her and she laughed.

"Jamie, I saw the most amazing thing last night." She tried to describe the lights, but felt like she failed miserably to convey their grandeur.

"I bet it's Martians," Jamie said happily.

"I'm glad I didn't think of that last night!"

The cold was penetrating even inside their little tent, so she took a deep breath and jumped out of bed. She tucked him back in. "I'll have it warm in here in a jiffy."

He looked at her trustingly.

She laid out the fire carefully, as she had last night, and struck a match to it. It flared up healthily, but she quickly realized something was dreadfully wrong. For some reason the smoke was belching back into the cabin. Within moments she could barely breathe.

She remembered it was smoke inhalation that killed, not fire, and she hustled Jamie out of bed and outside. The sky had an ominous gunmetal gray quality to it. She was aware she had no idea what cold really was. Even the chill of last night had not prepared her for this.

The cold bit into them as though it had fangs. She raced back in for jackets that were hopelessly inadequate against the ferocious cold.

"We'll just let the smoke clear," she said with authority, "and then I'll try to light the fire again." Her feeling of well-being from last night was dissipating completely. What if she couldn't get a fire going? What if the cabin remained ice-cold? What if she and Jamie froze to death, greenhorns in this great Canadian wilderness?

If things got that bad, she told herself, they could walk out. Half a day. She looked at Jamie rocking from one foot to another in his sneakers. Obviously the footwear was as hopelessly inadequate as their jackets. Would they have feet left if they walked half a day in this cold?

She heard the growl of a truck engine, and knew she felt exactly as pioneers had felt years ago when the fort was surrounded and they heard the far-off trumpet.

"Here comes the cavalry," she told Jamie.

He smiled at her. "No, it's not. It's Riley. I knew he'd come back."

Oh, sure, kid, when you have a request in with Santa anything can happen. She remembered the lights last night, and didn't feel nearly as cynical as she wanted to feel.

Not that, God forbid, she wanted to start thinking of Riley Keenan in the same light Jamie was thinking of him in.

By the time the truck came over the last little rise, and came to a halt, Beth's relief at being rescued had been overcome by her humiliation at needing rescuing. And they were less than twenty-four hours into their Christmas adventure.

Riley leaped out of the truck, leaving the door open. He came running toward them, his legs so strong and lean, all masculine grace and strength. It could make a woman weak if she let it.

Don't let it, she commanded herself.

"Are you okay?" He caught her shoulders between big hands, and she felt the pure power in his grasp, nodded, let the weakness wash over her, let his strength move into its place.

Thankfully his grasp lasted less than two seconds.

Unhesitatingly he went into the cabin. Moments later, he was throwing open windows. He came out with his arms full of blankets. He wrapped one quickly around Jamie, the other around her.

"It will just take a minute for the smoke to clear."

"What happened?" she said through chattering teeth.

"You forgot to open the damper on the stove."

"The damper?"

"It controls how much air gets at the fire. Lots

of air, hot fire. Less air, smoldering fire. No air, smoke."

"I didn't touch anything," she said defensively.

"You probably knocked it closed with your leg. I've done that myself on this stove. You're shaking." He pulled the blanket tighter around her, and then wrapped a solid arm around her shoulder. She felt his warmth seeping into her.

"Are you okay, Jamie?" he asked.

"Oh, yes. This is exciting! It's like on Oregon Trail, being a pioneer. That's a computer game at school. You have to collect all this stuff, and do all this stuff right, or you die." This was said with a certain innocent enthusiasm, and Riley burst out laughing.

She looked at him laughing, and felt her heart stop. The man was not just good-looking. He was absolutely extraordinary.

"What brings you up this way?" she asked. She had got the impression last night that he was clear of them.

"Oh, I was in the neighborhood," he said.

He'd been worried about her. She might have thought that was nice, if it wasn't a reflection on what he thought of her competence. The fact that his thoughts had been entirely accurate did not endear him to her, either.

"I would have figured out the damper."

"Auntie was nearly kidnapped by Martians last night," Jamie told Riley solemnly.

Riley looked like he found that as likely as her figuring out the damper. "Martians," he said with a little shake of his head, and a glance toward his truck.

Already sorry he'd come, tangled himself a little deeper with them.

Beth might have just accepted that sidelong look. But now she knew differently. Penny was looking out for her. And Penny would not accept a look like that slide by unchallenged.

"I am not a flake!" she said, defensively. "There were weird lights in the sky. And I didn't ever once think of Martians."

Jamie gave her a look that let her know he expected her loyalty in Martian theories.

"Come on. It's safe to go back inside." Riley's jaw was working, and he was trying not to look at her. He was going to laugh again. And at her expense this time.

"What's so funny?" she demanded.

"You didn't have a strange encounter of the third kind last night," he said.

"It was not my imagination! It was real."

"Yes, it was. The Northern Lights."

So, this vacation was not a complete write-off, after all. She could go home and tell her girlfriends in the office she had witnessed one of nature's most startling phenomena.

And that would not be his smile.

"Hey, something touched me," Jamie cried.

"Touched you?" And then she felt it, too. Wet, and cold, like the kiss of butterfly made of ice.

Jamie tilted back his head, and looked at the sky. She did the same.

It was full of huge, white feathers floating down.

"Snow!" Jamie cried.

"Snow," she whispered.

She noticed that Riley Keenan did not look nearly as pleased as she and Jamie did.

———————

Chapter 4

"Love letters from heaven," she murmured, as she watched Jamie turn ecstatic circles, his arms wide spread, trying to catch snowflakes. He stuck out his tongue and turned around and around.

"First Martians try to grab you and now heaven is sending you love letters? Lady Arizona, you are a flake."

Lady Arizona! "The Martians were Jamie's spin on things," she defended herself. "I never thought Martians were trying to grab me!" Beth cast a glance at Riley. That funny little smile was tickling his lips again. He was teasing her. And she didn't know what to do about it. Penny would tease him back.

"But you do believe heaven is sending you love letters?"

"Of course," she said, and stuck out her tongue. She tasted the snowflake. "That one was from Elvis."

He actually laughed.

Penny would have left it at that, but Beth hesitated. What did she care if Riley thought she was a nut? She tried not to care. She told herself she didn't care. But she cared.

"Jamie wanted snow for Christmas as proof that his mom was really watching out for him, his special angel, the way everybody keeps telling him." After the words were out, she realized such a statement hardly strengthened her case for not being a flake. Why had she told him that? It was so private. So personal. Why did she have this feeling, that underneath all the rough edges, Riley Keenan was really a man who could be trusted with anything?

She hoped he would have the good grace to drop it, but he was looking at her intently.

"Do you believe that?" he asked. "That she's watching over him? And over you, too?"

She wanted to make another flip remark, to hide her soul from him, but she found she was incapable of it. "It's what I want to believe most of all."

She waited for the cutting remark that would

tell her she had, once again, trusted unwisely, but it did not come.

After a long time, he said simply. "That's a nice thing to believe, Beth. I hope it's true." He was silent, and then he scanned the sky. Beth could not miss the faint worry etched in his brow.

"You're not seeing love letters," she said.

"I guess not."

"What are you seeing?"

He shrugged. "It could be trouble. There was a storm warning on the radio this morning. We don't get that much snow here, and when we do, it's usually drier, smaller flakes. But the weather report this morning said we were in for a real dump. A storm's brewing that could last until Christmas Eve. They're predicting more snow than we've seen in twenty years."

"Really?" she breathed. *Oh, Penny, you always did know how to send a love letter.*

"You don't seem to understand," he said in a low voice, so Jamie wouldn't hear. "You could get snowed in up here."

"What does that mean?"

"The road could become impassable. I put the snow blade on the front of my truck this morning when I heard the news, but it could take me days to get the road open. What if you missed your flight home?"

She really resented it that he was bringing all this

practical, but very negative information, to her attention. When she just wanted to enjoy the magic.

Magic would rate right up there with Martians for him.

"What do you suggest then?" she asked. Jamie was trying to lick a snowflake off the end of his nose with his tongue. It had been a long time since she had seem him look so joyous and carefree.

"I think," he said slowly, "you won't like the answer. We should get you out of here while we still can."

That was the problem with showing somebody your vulnerable side. It could so easily be mistaken for weakness. She said no in a tone that would have made Penny proud.

Naturally he acted like she hadn't said a thing. "There's a nice bed-and-breakfast in Bragg Creek. I'm sure they could find room for you in an emergency."

"Last night you scoffed at me for looking ahead and seeing emergencies."

His face was setting itself in dark forbidding lines. She shivered. He looked like a war chief, accustomed to giving commands, and being obeyed!

"I scoffed at you," he said, his patience obviously strained, "because you were indulging in fantasy emergencies! Bears and burglars! You don't know the reality of this country, but I do."

"Weather reports are quite as often fiction as

fact." She could feel the stubbornness taking up roost within her. She'd been an embarrassing pushover most of her life. Being stubborn felt wonderful.

He sighed heavily. He looked away. She could tell he was trying to keep his patience, that he was going to try to talk reason to the little woman.

And she was having none of it.

Her mind was made up. "I'm going to make breakfast now. I'm sure the cabin is aired out. Bacon and eggs, Jamie?"

"Yes, please. Riley, stay and have breakfast with us. Please?"

"I'm sure Riley's busy," she said, anxious to be rid of him since he was so eager to rain on her parade. Snow on her parade. Ruin her parade.

He obviously just wanted to go—but not without convincing her to abandon her Christmas cabin.

"I guess I could stop for breakfast," he said, as if he'd agreed to eating crushed glass and broken nails.

She rolled her eyes and went into the cabin after giving Jamie careful instructions about his perimeters for outside play. Inside, the smoke had cleared, though the smell of it clung. She shivered and began closing windows.

Riley came in behind her. He opened his mouth to speak, took one look at her face, and busied himself with the fire.

Finally someone was seeing her as a force to be reckoned with!

But residing inside her, right beside that force to be reckoned with, was an equally powerful force, that yearned for the quiet intimacy of this scene to be real. That wished she really was part of a family that was snowbound in this adorable little cabin for Christmas. That wished Riley would turn and look at her with laughter in his eyes, tenderness, instead of irritation, and impatience.

After he got the fire going to his satisfaction, Riley went and rustled around in the front hall closet, and came out with a box. He opened it, and she saw neatly folded children's winter clothes.

"If you're going to stay," he said, "you should at least know enough to keep him dry. Ever heard of hypothermia?"

So, he was conceding that they were staying, but he was not going to be graceful about it.

"Jamie, come here," he called from the front door. Out of the corner of her eye, she watched amused, as he picked Jamie up and popped him inside a one-piece snowsuit. In moments he had the little boy outfitted in a snowsuit and mittens, a scarf and a toque.

"Where'd that stuff come from?" she asked.

"My mom must have brought it up. It looks like all my old winter stuff."

Bethany tried to imagine him small, fitting into

the snowsuit he had just shoved Jamie into. It was a hard stretch.

Turning to the kitchen window she could see Jamie chasing snowflakes. Still smiling, she regarded the stove. Turn on the gas, light the match…

Poof.

She flew back from the stove. Riley was at her side in an instant.

"Singed your eyebrows," he said, touching one. "Look."

He took a mirror off the windowsill and held it up to her. Her eyebrows were frosted gray on the end, and so were her eyelashes.

Just her luck, sharing space with the most gorgeous man on earth and she looked like Rabbit off *Winnie the Pooh.*

"You have to light the match first," he told her, "then turn on the gas. This is exactly why you shouldn't stay here."

Exactly, she thought sadly. But that was not what she said. "Don't be ridiculous. Do you think I'm going to make that particular mistake again?"

"Look, Bethany, if that road snows in, I can't come and check on you."

"You weren't planning on coming and checking on me when you left here yesterday. I am twenty-six years old. I don't need checking on, for heaven's sake. You're not my baby-sitter."

"You were scared to stay here by yourself yesterday," he reminded her.

"I was tired." *I didn't believe in miracles the way I do now. I didn't believe in myself the way I do now.* Though, of course, believing in herself was a work in progress.

"Look, Bethany, I'm not questioning your competence—"

"Oh, right," she said, sending him a suspicious sidelong look. She did not like the tone of voice he was using. It was his sweet-talking tone of voice, and she bet he'd used it many, many times in his life to get women exactly where he wanted them.

She might have been more open to it herself if he was trying to steal a kiss, rather than trying to convince her to abandon ship.

She blushed at the thought that she would be open to being kissed by him, flipped an egg and sent him another look.

Well, the truth was she was a woman. And he was one heck of a man.

Not that she'd ever been the kind of woman men tried to steal kisses from. That had been Penny's department.

She wondered what Penny would have done if she found herself at such close quarters with a man who aggravated her and attracted her at the same time.

No doubt it wouldn't have been flipping eggs as though her life depended on it!

"I'm not questioning your competence," he said, again, his voice silky. "I realize this is brand-new territory for you. My mom wouldn't have given it a thought, because she's lived this kind of lifestyle forever. Woodstoves and propane appliances are nothing to her.

"But a city girl being left out here on her own during what could be the worst snowstorm in a quarter of a century would be irresponsible on my part. I know we'll refund you your money. That won't be a problem."

"I'm not leaving," she said. Penny would have left it at that, but she felt compelled to add, "Look at all the work your mother did on this cabin! How can I walk away from that? She baked us cookies! And bread."

"She'd understand, honestly. She didn't know we were about to have the Mount St. Helens of snowstorms."

"She *cared* about us," Bethany said stubbornly.

He was very silent. Finally he said, slowly and carefully, "Don't you have anybody to care about you?"

She had made herself sound pathetic. And she had been way more personal than she wanted to be. Again.

"I just meant it's been a long time since someone looked after me," she clarified.

"You can take the cookies with you," he said hopefully. "And the bread."

How could men be so stupid? It wasn't about the bread and cookies. It was about the *feeling*. Mind you, he did look like the man least likely to be able to call his feelings by name.

"It would be a terrible shame if nobody enjoyed this cabin at Christmas," she said firmly. "Criminal."

"Criminal is marching into a bank with a sawed off shotgun," he told her. "This is just doing the sensible thing. The practical thing."

"I guess we define criminal differently."

"Some definitions are not open to debate. Do you think you're going to find 'Abandoning the Christmas Cabin' as a heading in the Criminal Code? No, you aren't."

"I hate it when people ask questions, and then answer themselves."

"I hate it when people won't listen to reason."

"Good," she said. "We have something in common. We hate each other."

She heard a small whimper and turned to see Jamie standing in the doorway, a layer of white melting on his new snowclothes.

"You can't! You can't hate each other. You can't!"

Her nephew's distress was so real. Of course she was not allowed to hate the daddy material!

"Jamie," she said patiently, "I don't hate Riley,

really. It's just an expression. I don't know Riley well enough to hate him." *Yet.*

"You don't hate my auntie, do you?" Jamie asked Riley.

"Of course not."

"You like her, don't you?"

Riley looked like he'd been backed into a bear trap. "Sure," he said shortly.

"That's good," Jamie said, then to Buddy Bear, in an undertone that Beth nevertheless heard. "That is very, very good. Is breakfast ready?"

"Ten minutes."

"I'll be outside. I'm looking for the perfect Christmas tree."

"Your mother said we could cut one down," she told Riley before he could protest. She watched Jamie skip out the door.

"Not too far," she called after him.

Jamie laughed. "The front yard is *full* of trees." The door slammed behind him.

For months she had been begging Jamie to go outside and play with his friends. For months he had sat in front of the TV hugging Buddy Bear, saying he didn't feel like playing.

She put some bacon in the pan, and loved the sizzle and smell. "Nothing makes a place feel like home as much as frying a little bacon."

"This is not your home. You are leaving. For your own safety, and for my sanity—"

She turned and looked at him. "Do you hear that sound, Riley Keenan?"

He stopped, midsentence, baffled. "Sound?"

"Listen." She opened the window.

He cocked his head. "You mean Jamie laughing?"

She nodded. "That's what I mean. We are not leaving this place, not when it can make him laugh like that. We are not leaving the place that is giving him back his joy. We are eating breakfast and then we are going to cut down our Christmas tree. I don't care if we get snowed in for a month. We are not leaving. Do you hear me?"

There. She had not even had to mention magic and miracles.

It was quiet. She turned and looked at him. He was regarding her silently, looking somewhat stunned. She suspected it had been a long time since anyone had told him how things were going to be.

"Yes, ma'am," he said finally, "I guess I hear you."

"Good. Sunny-side, or over easy?"

The problem with women, Riley thought as he ate his bacon and eggs, was that they based decisions on sentiment rather than reason. Given this rather large difference in the way men and women approached life, he was amazed that the human species survived.

Five years ago, it hadn't mattered that the house was built and the invitations on order. *It wasn't fun anymore.* He had scars. He sensed, deeper, that Alicia had been furiously and unforgivingly angry with him.

Because he hadn't listened to her.

Don't go in there! Are you crazy? For God's sake, Riley...

"Are you all right? Riley?"

He came back to the present, and felt embarrassed at how completely he had slipped away. Beth was looking at him, mildly concerned.

"Sorry," he said, "I was thinking of something else."

She was still looking at him, her brow faintly furrowed. It occurred to him that Beth Cavell was Alicia's polar opposite. It went deeper than the surface differences, though those were many.

Alicia had loved makeup and had known how to use it. Beth's face was fresh-scrubbed and makeup free. Alicia had dyed her hair, blond, of course. Blondes have more fun, she'd tell him. Oh, yeah, fun had been important to her, as he had been about to find out.

Alicia had dressed to show off every asset she had, and she had many; Beth dressed like one of those nuns who didn't wear a habit. Today, she had pulled on a prim long-sleeved blouse, that looked like it had been freshly pressed, even though he knew it had to have come out of a suitcase, over top of the pajamas he'd caught her in.

It was as if she thought her pajamas were indecent. In actual fact they looked like she had picked them up in kids' wear, red flannel pajamas with candy canes on them.

Alicia had liked red, too, but she could have shown Beth a thing or two about indecent. Her idea of pajamas had been film and lace. He was aware, as the thought flashed through his mind, that he did not even have the slightest physical ache at the thought of Alicia at her sexiest, which had been mighty sexy.

Most of all, though, Beth's eyes were different than Alicia's. It was not just that they were a different color, though he did not think he would ever see that shade of green again, but a different spirit shone in them.

Alicia had been high energy, flash and fire.

Beth's eyes were calm and soft and kind.

"More bacon?" she said.

Maybe as a man got older, he put value in different things. Alicia had been an orchid, wild and exotic. Beth was more like a marigold. And he was amazed by how appealing he found that. So more bacon would be a big mistake.

He got up. "No, thanks, I should go."

She had made up her mind. She was a grown-up. He was not responsible for her.

"Auntie Mommy, are you ready to chop down the Christmas tree?"

"Of course," she said. "I'm not even going to do the dishes. We'll get the tree organized before we do one other thing."

Riley was aware of admiring her slightly. The dishes could wait while she wove Christmas magic around a little boy.

Though, if he were honest, she was being sentimental instead of practical again. In an hour or two the egg would be hardened on, the pan would be congealed.

"I can do the tree," he said, and then couldn't believe he had said it.

No, no, no! He'd sworn off Christmas trees, and Christmas and all things cheerful. He had.

"Thank you, but no," she said stubbornly. "You can be on your way. Jamie and I can manage quite well."

Riley did not miss the dirty look Jamie gave her. "I want Riley to stay and help with the tree." He turned and smiled at Riley. "We always have hot chocolate with real whip cream when we decorate it. And Auntie Mommy makes popcorn strings."

"I can't stay for that part. I just meant I'd cut down the tree. It can be harder than it looks."

"I can manage," she said tersely.

Now the stubborn was coming out in him. How

did she know she could manage? Had she ever chopped down a tree before?

"How about if I just watch then?" he said silkily. "You know, in case of emergency? I wouldn't want you to chop off your toe and have to walk out. That would probably take more than half a day."

Jamie laughed.

"You are not funny," she told Riley haughtily.

"I think you're pretty funny," Jamie whispered to him, when she disappeared with the box of winter clothes into her bedroom.

"Thanks. Us guys gotta stick together."

Jamie looked very pleased about that. "Yeah. Us guys got to stick together. I've never had a guy to stick together with before, just Mommy and Auntie Mommy."

"Doesn't Auntie Mommy have a boyfriend?" Riley realized he should feel ashamed of himself for prying information out of a child, but he didn't.

"She used to. He didn't like me."

"Then he was an ass," Riley said, only he didn't stop at ass.

Jamie nodded vigorously. "Yes, he was an ass." He didn't stop at ass, either, thoroughly enjoying this fraternity of males. "Him and Auntie Mommy were supposed to get married, only they didn't."

"A story I know well."

"Do you?" Jamie looked puzzled.

"Sorry. I didn't mean that the way it sounded."

"I'm not supposed to know, but Sam didn't want me. He wanted babies of his own. A family of his own. I listened from the hall closet the night he told Auntie Mommy."

Ah, so that's why Auntie Mommy was a million miles from home at Christmas.

"And Auntie Mommy told him to find a high cliff and leap off it, didn't she?"

Jamie nodded with satisfaction.

"Good for her. I would have done the same thing."

"Really? Do you think I would be a nice little boy to have? Just as good as babies of your own?"

"Oh, way better," Riley said. "You're past the stinky stage."

Jamie chortled happily over that, and then got out of his chair, came around the table and climbed right in Riley's lap.

Jeez, Riley thought, *I didn't say I was going to adopt you.* He should have thought of an excuse to get the kid off his lap, but he couldn't think of one.

The child's trust in him, his *liking* for him, when he knew himself to be anything but likable was baffling. And just a little bit nice, too.

Beth came back into the room. "Jamie, I'm sure Riley doesn't need you on his lap. He's not a piece of furniture."

Ah. Auntie very wisely did not want the little boy getting too attached to him.

"He said I would be a nice little boy to have," Jamie said stubbornly.

"That's only because he hasn't seen the bathtub after you get out of it," she said, lightly, but Riley heard something forced in her voice, saw anxiety in her eyes when she looked over Jamie's head at him.

He put the boy off his lap. "Let's go get that Christmas tree before Santa notices one of his elves is missing and swoops down to get your aunt Beth."

"That bad, huh?"

She did look ridiculously like an elf. She had on a hat his mother had made for him one Christmas that looked like a court jester's hat. He had never worn it.

Then she had on a too-large jacket, and a thick pair of ski pants, one red mitten and one green one, and snowmobile boots that were way too large.

They went out the door, and he noticed, uneasily, that it had snowed a great deal in a very short amount of time. There looked to be about two inches accumulated on the ground already. He scanned the sky. And lots more to come.

"Here's the tree chopper-downer," Jamie said to his aunt.

Riley folded his arms over his chest and watched as she tried to pull the ax from out of the piece of wood it had been wedged in.

After letting her struggle longer than was strictly

gentlemanly, he went and one-armed it out of the stump.

"Show-off," she said nastily.

"Wait until you try chopping down the tree," he said, just as nastily.

"Which tree, Jamie?"

Jamie raced to the edge of the wood. He had picked a lovely, perfectly shaped blue spruce. It was about eight feet high, and the base of it was no more than six inches across.

An easy tree to fell.

"Stand back," she ordered. She took a deep breath, and set her feet. And then she swung mightily at the trunk of the tree.

She hit it, and he could tell the reverberation of the ax biting into the wood took her by surprise. The snow fell from the limbs and went straight down her neck. She did an amusing little snow-out-of-intimate places dance, then with great panting, she pulled the ax free, and swung again.

She hit the tree in a totally different place, inches above her first mark.

Jamie cast Riley a worried look. "How long does it take to cut down a Christmas tree?"

"That depends," he said, "how long a person can be foolishly stubborn for. It could take all day."

"It will not," she said.

He shrugged. With the snow falling so hard, he should be eager to go. He knew that. But somehow, he suddenly didn't mind if it did take her all day. He *wanted* to know how stubborn she was.

It was plenty stubborn. Jamie grew restless. "Do you know how to make snow angels?" he asked, tugging on Riley's hand. "I saw it on TV once."

"Oh, sure. You just lie down in the snow, and sweep your hands up over your head and back down, and your feet, too."

Jamie looked baffled.

"Like this," he said, not believing he was going to demonstrate. Unlike his guests who were dressed for sub-Arctic conditions, he was wearing jeans and a jean jacket. Nonetheless, if you were asked to demonstrate the ancient Canadian cultural art of making snow angels, what could you do?

He lay down, and demonstrated, stood up very carefully and jumped out of the indent in the snow.

Jamie inspected the snow angel with careful reverence. Riley glanced over to see Beth watching him, that same faintly anxious look on her face as when Jamie had been on his knee.

He watched Jamie make an angel, looked at it carefully and nodded gravely. "Perfect," he proclaimed.

Such a simple thing to make a child's face shine like that! Jamie was off, creating whole congregations of snow angels.

"Hey, you're looking at me like you've figured out I'm no angel," he said, moving over to her, surreptitiously examining her progress on the tree. The trunk was badly mangled, but the tree showed little sign of being about to fall.

"Be careful of Jamie," she said in a low voice, not looking at him.

"Be careful of him, how? He's sick? He shouldn't be in the snow making angels?"

"Oh, no, nothing like that, thank God."

He could see the struggle on her face. She took another swing at the tree, so tired the blade didn't even bite, but bounced back.

Enough was enough. He took the ax from her grasp. She didn't protest, either. She kind of pretended it hadn't happened, so he took a swing.

She pretended that wasn't happening, either.

"Riley, he doesn't have many male influences in his life. He could develop a case of hero worship."

He turned and looked at her so swiftly, he nearly caught himself in the leg with the ax. He detected, from the uncomfortable look on her face, that she was speaking in half-truths.

So, what was the rest of the truth? That she had already figured out he was no hero? Completely unworthy of a five-year-old's worship?

Since he already knew that, why did he feel this strange little pang in his gut?

He watched Jamie flopping in the snow, spreading his arms and legs wide. An angel. A real live one.

"Okay," he said, a military commander in need

of a strategy. "I'll get the tree down, and help you drag it into the cabin. Then I'm out of here."

"I didn't mean to hurt your feelings," she said in a low voice.

Hurt his feelings? As if! But was that what that little pang in his chest was? A hurt feeling.

"My feelings aren't hurt," he said.

She went on, just as if he had said his feelings *were* hurt, "There's no point him getting attached to you, that's all. We're not staying that long."

"I'm not staying that long," he shot back. "Five more minutes."

The tree came down in five swings, his strength fueled by desperation to be out of this awkward situation. He hauled it to the door, and leaned it up against the frame.

"Well," he said, "time to go. Look at that snow! Merry Christmas."

Ho, ho, ho, and let me outta here.

"How's my auntie going to make the tree stand up?" Jamie asked him, his hands on his hips. "She can't even make the tree stand up at home, and it's not even real."

"I'll figure it out," Beth assured Jamie. "Riley has to go now."

Yes, he did have to go. Jamie looked upset that he was leaving, already far more attached to him than he had a right to be.

On the other hand, Riley had just seen how she

had "figured out" how to use the ax. Bethany Cavell could be dangerous.

He sure as hell didn't want to be anybody's hero. He'd already tried that gig, and hated it.

But he wasn't prepared to leave a poor orphaned kid with a tree that was very likely to fall on top of his only living relative and spoil Christmas for him forever and for all time.

He sighed.

"I'll put up the tree. Then I'm going. And I mean it."

Jamie was smiling as if he didn't mean it at all.

Chapter 5

Riley wrestled the tree through the door. It was bigger than it had seemed like it was outside. It was also a fine finishing touch on the Christmas atmosphere his mother had worked so hard to create, if a person was susceptible to such things.

Even a person who was not could see that the arrival of the tree made the cabin seem like more than a cabin.

Like a place where magic might happen.

Even more than that, like a home.

This was not his *home,* he reminded himself. It was not anybody's home. It was a hunting cabin impersonating a home.

He dragged the tree by its trunk into the living room, not even a little guilty about the trail of needles and snow he was leaving behind him.

The reality of the tree was that it was going to make a mess. The reality was he had never had to worry about a little dirt and debris on the cabin floor before, and he wasn't going to start now.

Or at least he might not have started, if Beth wasn't already coming behind him with a broom and a dustpan.

"Where do you want it?"

"What do you think, Jamie? In that corner?"

Riley hauled the tree over to the corner, and shoved it upright. It swatted him in the face with a branch. In consideration of the company he was keeping, he bit back the first word that came to his mind, but he deeply resented the fact that he had to.

Jamie looked at the placement of the tree critically. "Not there," he decided.

Or there, or there, or there. After what felt to be several thousand moves of the tree, Jamie decided it looked best in front of the window.

Riley glanced at his watch. Somehow another half hour had trickled by. He looked suspiciously at Jamie. Was the kid trying to keep him here?

Jamie gazed back at him, his blue eyes huge and innocent, which made Riley feel guilty for suspecting guile.

Beth, unlike her nephew, seemed unaware Riley

was still attached to the tree. She was looking at it intently, her hands on her hips, tilting her head this way and that.

Riley became uncomfortably aware of her. She looked less demure with the rosy blush of the chilly outdoor air on her cheeks. Her eyes were sparkling, as if she thought setting up a Christmas tree rated really high in the thrilling-things-to-do department.

"A little to the left," she said, as if she was hanging a Van Gogh at a gallery. "And could you turn it just a touch? There's a little bare spot there."

And then she blushed as if she was talking about her own naked flesh, instead of a place on a spruce tree.

He complied, but the blush had made his mind take a wayward turn. He wondered if she was a virgin. The renegade thought caused him great embarrassment, and he placed his head behind a few branches, so he could watch her without her being aware evil thoughts were filling his head.

The placement of his head reminded him why he always encouraged his mother to choose a pine instead of a spruce.

Spruce was way too prickly. A perfect match for his personality.

"Right there," Jamie finally decided. "It's the most beautiful tree in the world. Isn't it, Riley? Isn't it?"

Jamie seemed to be missing the prickly part of both the tree and the man.

"It's okay," Riley said, stubbornly.

"Perfect," Beth insisted.

The problem with the male mind was once it started down a certain track it was hard to rope it back in.

He was thinking how much he'd like to hear the word *perfect* from her in a very different context.

No wonder she had spotted the fact he was a totally unsuitable hero for her nephew in such short order.

"Jamie, come on," she said, holding out her hand, "We'll get some popcorn going and start the strings, while Riley sets up the tree."

"No," Jamie said stubbornly, ignoring her hand, and folding his arms manfully over his small chest. "Us guys will set up the tree."

Riley didn't miss the look on her face. "A three-minute job," he assured her. Not long enough for *attachments* to form.

Riley, with his little shadow close behind him, went outside to the crawl space under the cabin. He found some two-by-six lumber and located some old tools he had stored in the same spot.

"Hell," he said. "A porcupine's been under here. It looks like he's nearly eaten the handle off the hammer." Porcupines were notorious for liking the salt that sweaty palms left behind on ax and hammer handles.

"A real porcupine? Where is he? I want to see him," Jamie declared, looking around eagerly.

"No, you don't want to see him," Riley told him. "Real porcupines are not pets. Do you have a soft spot for prickly things or something?"

"I guess I do," Jamie said, a touch stubbornly. He continued looking around hopefully for the porcupine.

"Look, he left you a quill." Riley picked it up and handed it to him. "Don't stick yourself with it. And if you and your aunt see that critter, you stay away. Porcupines are not friendly. Not even a little bit." And frankly, the boy's friendliness gauge was not functioning.

Jamie took the quill with the reverence Riley might have expected of Arthur receiving the sword, Excalibur.

When they went back into the cabin, Riley stood for a moment in the doorway, and not just to kick the snow off his boots, either. The smell of the tree was overwhelming in the small cabin, and now it was mixing with the smell of popping corn.

For a place that was not a home, the illusion was becoming overpowering.

He took a quick glance in the kitchen. Sure enough, she had cut open the microwave bags of popping corn, and was doing it manually.

Beth was standing at the stove, shaking the pop-corn as if her life depended on it. At least she had managed to turn on the stove without blowing her-self up. He should consider that a good thing. She didn't need him anymore.

Still, she looked soft and feminine and whole-some, the kind of woman a man with brains dreamed of coming home to someday.

Luckily for him, he already knew he didn't have much in the way of brains, and even less in the way of dreams.

Still, Riley felt a moment of almost unbearable longing, a wish inside of him that was brand-new, and yet age-old at the same time.

The simple wish of a man not to be alone.

"Come on," he said roughly, setting up a work station on the floor in front of the tree, "let's get at it." With Jamie watching him with interest that should have been reserved for the assembly of a space shuttle, Riley shaped a rough *X* for the tree stand.

He was going to slam it together—a three-minute job after all—when he glanced up and saw the look on Jamie's face.

A look so full of hope and wistfulness that it could gentle a porcupine.

"I guess you'd like to try this," Riley said reluc-tantly, and sat back on his haunches. He was rewarded with an ear-to-ear grin. He sighed inwardly, and started the nail.

He surrendered the mauled hammer to Jamie, then let him pound the nail in. He watched as Jamie, both hands on the hammer, tongue between his teeth, took careful aim and tapped the nail.

"Hell," Jamie said when he missed the nail, then he and Riley both shot a look at his aunt, who was obviously being deafened by the sound of corn popping.

"Maybe you shouldn't say that word," Riley suggested in an undertone.

"You say it," Jamie pointed out without looking up from the hammer.

I am not used to being an example to small boys. "That doesn't make it right."

"It makes it right by me."

"Okay. I won't say it anymore," Riley said. It felt, somehow, like he'd been blackmailed into that concession. It made it worse that he'd been successfully blackmailed by someone three feet high. And guileless.

"Okay, I won't, either."

At least, Riley thought, he had probably held off the wrath of Beth for the next three minutes until he made his getaway.

But it soon occurred to Riley, with all this help, this wasn't going to be a three-minute job, after all.

Tap, tap, miss, miss, miss, tap, miss, tap, tap. The

nail began to bend over crooked and Riley took the hammer and straightened it, resisted the temptation to whack the nail into place himself. Instead he returned the hammer to Jamie.

It amazed Riley that he was capable of such patience.

But even more amazing to him was the funny swelling in his chest that these simple moments were giving him. He wondered if fathers, who did these small things with their boys every day, knew what a privilege it was to be the one guiding those first clumsy efforts that would slowly grow into the skills and strengths that made a man.

Again, he felt a strange ache. Loss. Loneliness. The road not chosen. Uncomfortable thoughts, ones he couldn't wait to get away from.

Still, he forced himself to study Jamie's finished effort carefully, turning the Christmas tree stand over in his hands. This also was new to his world—to put the boy's needs ahead of his own.

"That's good," he said with a nod.

Jamie looked like he'd received a medal.

Riley wondered, uneasily, who was in danger of getting attached to whom, here. The air was warm, sweet with the smells of spruce, and popcorn.

He and Jamie finished the stand quickly and with great fanfare nailed it to the bottom of the tree.

"Ta-da" Jamie called as they stood it up.

Riley let go of the tree. It rocked unsteadily.

After several attempts to get it to sit flatter on the floor, Riley gave up.

He hauled a chair over to the tree, and with a piece of stout string, wrapped the main trunk and nailed it to the wall. There. No danger, now, of the tree falling over on the orphan or the orphan's aunt.

His work here was through.

He got down off the chair. Beth had come in, and was looking at the tree. She crossed her arms over her chest, and tried to hide a smile, but didn't quite succeed.

"What?" he said defensively.

"Oh, I was just thinking, it's just like home," she said. "I usually end up doing the string thing to our tree every year, too."

"You have an artificial tree," he pointed out, as if that made her failing greater than his.

He had to get out of here. He was letting his manhood feel threatened by whether of not he could set up a Christmas tree as well as a wee slip of a woman—who had never even had a real Christmas tree before!

"Do you want hot chocolate? And popcorn?"

His mouth watered. It was a test. He had to pass it, or he would be lost forever. "No." He remembered he was being an example, whether he wanted to be one or not. "Uh, thanks, anyway."

"Please, Riley?" Jamie said. "I'll give you my marshmallow."

Seldom had he been offered such riches. He swayed, but did not fall.

"No, I can't." He hardened his heart to the look of disappointment on the child's face. "I have to go. The snow. The road. You know."

It was obvious Jamie did not know, but his aunt did. For the good of everyone here, he had to go.

"Thanks for the tree," she said softly.

"And the snow angels," Jamie said, and his easy forgiveness felt like as much a gift as the offer of marshmallows. "And for letting me help."

Such a simple thing to let him help. And yet there was a deep and satisfied glow on the child's face.

Riley glanced at Beth and saw the tenderness soften her features when she looked at her nephew. He wondered, a renegade thought, what it would be like to be loved by someone like her.

He had to get out of here. Too many traps, all around him. Good smells, the softness of a woman and the worship of a child.

Not the time to think of Beth and Jamie being here all alone for Christmas. It was her choice. He remembered asking her if they didn't have somewhere else to spend Christmas and the look on her face. Transparent.

Obviously if they had people to care about them—a large, extended family waiting with open arms and eggnog—they would not be up here.

By themselves.

A lonely little family at Christmas. He suspected they were in search of a miracle of some kind.

He could not help them with loneliness, and certainly not with miracles. He could be the most help to them by leaving now.

Before attachments developed.

"Okay," he said, all business, gathering up the tools to shove back under the cabin, and his coat, so he had no excuse to make a return trip inside the cabin. "You've got everything, straight, right? You know where the damper is? You know you have to light the match before you turn on the gas with the stove?"

"I got it," she said, and looked amused.

Well, why wouldn't she? He sounded like his mother.

Under the amusement, was she just a little bit sorry to be seeing him go? No, a trick of his imagination.

He turned around and bolted out the door. He told himself not to look at Jamie, not even one little glance, but as he was slipping on his jacket, his eyes accidentally went over there.

The little boy was silent, but his eyes reminded Riley of a big, old dog he used to have. It adored him, and his eyes followed him endlessly, always begged for just the smallest scraps of attention. Affection.

He practically ran out the door, tossed the tools

under the cabin, noted the snow was now nearly at his ankles. His truck was buried under a wet blanket of the white stuff.

Without bothering to clear the windows, he climbed in, and started the engine, let the wipers struggle under the heavy burden of the snow. When a patch was clear enough to see out of he did a neat U-turn in front of the cabin and headed down the road.

Jamie stood, his nose pressed against the window, waving. Riley hesitated, and then waved back. No need to worry about forming attachments now.

The wheels spun treacherously in hollows where the snow had gathered. On one small rise, he had to put the four-wheel-drive mechanism into four low to get up the other side.

That worried him. There was a chance that he was leaving those people on their own. That he wouldn't be able to get back in here for a few days.

It was one thing to tell himself she was an adult, that he had offered her an out and she had refused it.

It was quite another to be driving away from them when he was not at all convinced they knew what the reality could be up here.

What if it turned really cold? Not this nice, mild stuff, but the thirty or forty below stuff? You didn't want to let a fire go out in the middle of the night if that happened. And did they know better than to go outside if the mercury dropped below a certain level? Did they know just how quickly exposed skin could freeze if the wind came up?

How would they know that? They were from Arizona.

Okay, he told his conscience, *if it gets that cold, I'll come back up.* If the road was impassable he could always dress for an Arctic front and head up on his snowmobile. Jamie would like the snow machine.

A little picture danced through his mind, of flying around the cabin on the snowmobile. But it wasn't Jamie he pictured riding behind him.

He banished that thought, scowled at the road with the full intensity of his concentration for a full twenty or thirty seconds.

And then he wondered, what if they decided to try out that old sled he'd seen leaning up behind the back of the cabin? His mother must have put it there for them.

Hadn't his mom seen the article in the local paper about sledding accidents? At the time, he'd scanned it only briefly, and thought it was a waste of paper, a case of news being created where none really existed.

Who ever got hurt on a toboggan?

Well, according to that article, plenty of people. People who had been playing in snow all their lives, too. If people who had been riding sleds since they were babies could get hurt, what about those two sun bunnies from Arizona?

She's cautious, he told himself. *She'd never get up the guts to go fast enough to let either of them get hurt.*

The road got another twenty seconds of his attention.

What if the porcupine came back, and she heard it rustling around under the cabin and it scared her? What if Jamie tried to touch it?

What if in the excitement of Christmas she turned the propane on the stove, and forgot to light the match first? Turned on the propane and let it build a little too long before adding the match? She could catch her hair on fire. And what was the kid going to do then?

A poor kid who had already dealt with a whole lot more than he ever should have?

"Nothing's going to go wrong," he told himself, annoyed. "The porcupine is not coming back and the propane is not blowing up."

He was not generally a worrier. And yet he could not rid himself of the anxiety that was at the pit of his stomach.

It was the Christmas thing, he admitted to himself, finally. Some shadow left on his soul from that Christmas fire, where he had tried so hard.

And failed so completely.

Not completely, a voice tried to tell him, but he

was having none of it. Three children. And he had only gotten two of them.

So this anxious feeling, this feeling of impending disaster, had nothing to do with Beth and Jamie. It was his Christmas feeling. That was all. Other people had joy and happiness and good cheer for their Christmas feelings, and he did not.

For him it was that bleak time of year when trees and tinsel and lights and music triggered his darkest memories.

But what if the feeling that sat like a rock in his gut right now wasn't really about that? What if what he was writing off as an old anxiety revisiting was really some sort of premonition for the future?

"Premonition?" he growled out loud, and snorted in self-disgust. "Next thing you know, cowboy, you'll have an ad on TV telling people you'll do readings for them."

He knew as soon as he felt the truck start to slide that he hadn't been focusing nearly enough on the road. It was the kind of day where driving required one hundred per cent focus, and at best he had been giving it half of that.

He had come into that sharp bend in the road, just before it turned down into Caitlin Creek, just a mite too quickly. The big truck was now ignoring his attempts to wrestle it back onto the track, sliding stubbornly in a straight line.

The truck sailed majestically across the road,

plowed through drifted snow, and for a second, on the edge of the embankment, it hesitated, and Riley thought he might be able to hold it.

But then it teetered, and slowly slid on over. It bumped a few feet down and came to a rest, nose buried in snow, back tires up the slope.

He sat for a minute contemplating this development, and not liking it one little bit. He had lost his focus, lost his edge.

He simply *never* did that. He'd worked around big animals and machinery too long. He'd deliberately chosen a life where a man had to focus on what was in front of him, where there was a price to pay for a moment's inattention, for a mind that drifted to things past, or hopes future.

Resigned, he opened up his door and hopped out. The snow had drifted in piles here, and was deep. He slogged around the truck, and looked underneath it, surveying for damage. The slide had happened very slowly, embarrassingly so. It had made him believe he was really going to be able to stop the truck from going off the road.

Still, if he was looking for things to be grateful for—which he really wasn't—it looked as if, because of the slow motion ride into the ditch, his truck was unscathed. Stuck, to be sure, but unscathed.

He regarded the landscape and realized he could winch the truck out of here. But winch it out of here for what purpose? To slide off the road again, later? Miles from both the cabin and his house? Now, at least he was only a fifteen or twenty minute walk from the cabin.

The road was nearly impassable now. If the snow kept up, what could that mean by nightfall? By tomorrow morning?

The universe had handed him an excuse to go back and do the right thing. To make sure Beth and Jamie got safely through Christmas.

Maybe, the universe was even giving him a chance to make amends for a Christmas Eve a long time ago.

When one child had not made it to safety.

And it haunted him still.

"The cabin feels different when he's not here," Jamie said. He had a hot chocolate and marshmallow moustache and was carefully putting a popcorn string in the lower branches of the tree.

Beth wanted to tell Jamie not to be so silly, but the truth was she knew exactly what he meant. She felt Riley's absence nearly as intensely as she had felt his presence.

It felt like the life had whooshed out of the cabin when he had.

Why? It's not as if he was a cheerful sort. She supposed it was because he had that quality that could be called presence. He carried himself with a certain masculine confidence that could not be ignored. Energy crackled in the air around him.

Riley Keenan had a way of being that went beyond words to something else.

Spirit.

Riley Keenan had strength of spirit. So much so that when he left a room it seemed suddenly empty. As if the life force had all gone from it.

A voice inside her head told her she was kidding herself. What she missed was not his spirit. Or his presence.

The man was simply so damnably sexy it took a girl's breath away. He filled a room so completely it was hard to think of anything else when he was in it.

She had learned you could pop corn and think of how a guy's butt filled out his blue jeans. And notice the easy ripple of muscle as he wrestled trees and wielded axes. Or patiently showed a child how to hammer a nail.

Oh, no, it was a good thing he was gone. An absolute blessing.

"He's coming back," Jamie said.

"No, he isn't."

"Auntie, he's coming back."

She went and dropped on her knee beside Jamie, gathered him to her. How was she going to make him understand some requests were beyond Santa?

Was now the time to admit she had read that let-

ter? To tell Jamie she knew what his greatest hope
was, and that it just wasn't going to happen?

Did unfilled requests to Santa scar children for
life? Did the snow that she had traveled so far to
obtain for him count for anything at all?

"Jamie, if he doesn't come back, don't be too
disappointed, okay?"

He squirmed out of her embrace and went to the
window. "I'm not wishing he was coming back,"
Jamie told her. "I saw him. Walking along the road."

She joined Jamie at the window. Sure enough,
Riley Keenan was a dot in the distance. But even
at a distance it was easy to see his stride was long-
legged and powerful. He kicked up the snow in
clouds in front of him, but it did not shorten his
stride. He was a man at ease with himself, and with
the elements. He was a man who owned the earth.

Not to mention sexy.

As he drew closer, she could feel her heart beat-
ing in her chest.

"I don't have a Christmas present for him," Jamie
said, worriedly. "Do you?"

"He surely won't be here for Christmas. He's had
a problem with his truck. He's probably just coming back to—"

To what? Use the phone? There wasn't one.

"—to get a piece of wire or something," she finished weakly. Weakly, because a truth was making
itself known to her.

It made life way more complicated that he was coming back. Uncomfortable, even. He made her feel like a plain schoolgirl wanting to be noticed by the captain of the football team. He made her nerves sing with awareness. He made her blush. He made her stumble over her words.

And none of those things mattered. Somewhere deep in her heart, Beth was glad he was coming back. Trying not to appear at all eager, she waited until she heard him stamping off his boots on the step before she went and opened the door for him.

She planned on saying something pleasant, amused, sophisticated. Penny would have said, *Fancy meeting you here.*

But instead, when Beth opened the door, everything glib fled her mind, and she just stood there, swept away by his energy all over again.

"Truck went off the road," he said, as if he didn't notice she was staring at him.

"Oh my God, are you hurt?"

She realized, too late, it sounded like she cared too much.

"No," he said, smiling slightly, "it would take more than that to hurt me."

"You must be freezing." She stepped back from the door, and he stepped by her in a cloud of cold air.

That smelled heavenly.

"Actually I'm not too bad. In this country we're

always prepared in the winter, for breakdowns or in case we hit the ditch. I had snow boots, and a warmer jacket behind the seat."

"Are you staying for Christmas?" Jamie asked, jumping up and down, thrilled at the prospect.

"I guess that depends how long it snows," he said.

And then she understood the implications of his coming back. He hadn't come back to report to them he was off the road. Or to ask them for help. What help would she and Jamie be able to offer, after all?

He had come back because they were snowed in. Together.

Flustered, she turned away from him. "If you're hungry I have some soup ready for lunch."

"And after lunch, you can help me decorate the tree," Jamie told him. "I have the popcorn strings on. Come and see." He was tugging at Riley's hand.

Riley, not without reluctance, followed him in to the living room. "That looks nice," he said, mostly because Jamie seemed to expect him to say something.

"Will you help me finish decorating it, after lunch?" Jamie pleaded.

"I guess so."

Jamie seemed thrilled with the response, but Beth knew Riley was not interested in Christmas trees. Or stranded women or little boys. They were on his path, and he had stumbled upon them, but this was not the choice he had made.

He was just trying to make the best out of bad circumstances.

She wondered if Santa Claus had a sense of humor. Really, this was so unfair, that she should be snowed in in this delightful little cabin with this teeth-grindingly sexy man who did not like Christmas or anything that went with it.

It was so unfair.

And it was just about the most exciting thing that had ever happened to her.

Chapter 6

"This is my baby ball," Jamie told Riley. "See? It has my name on it and the year I was born, and it says Baby's First Christmas. I'd like it up near the top there."

Jamie had quickly caught on that their unexpected Christmas companion had the advantage of being able to reach the highest branches of their tree without needing a chair to assist him.

It was Bethany who felt disappointed. Considering she had an expectation that this tall, dark and very handsome stranger being dropped on her cabin doorstep was going to somehow be exciting, she could feel a little worm of discontent in her.

Riley, never outspoken, had become remote over lunch. Polite, but not quite there. She got the sensation that he felt, somehow, that he was fulfilling an obligation. Why would he feel that way? He had slid off the road. Why was he sending the silent message it was their fault that he was back here? Did he think if he'd gotten away sooner, it might not have happened?

He was stuck here, but he managed to be removed at the very same time, the body in the chair, the mind a million miles away.

But if she thought he had been quiet and removed over lunch, Riley was becoming increasingly more distant as they decorated the tree. She glanced at him now, and could see the remoteness in his features, a muscle flicking along his jaw as if he were grinding his teeth.

"You know," she told him, quietly, "this is supposed to be fun. I know you probably have a million more thrilling things to be doing, but you can't go anywhere, anyway. Why not make the most of it?"

He looked at her, surprised that she had read his mood. "More thrilling things to do?" he said. "No. It's not that. I just don't much get into the Christmas spirit."

"No kidding."

"Look, I'm sorry it shows. I'm doing my best not to be a wet blanket for you and the kid." Then his face brightened.

"You're right," he said. Visibly relieved, for a split second she thought he was going to throw himself wholeheartedly into the concept of having fun.

Ha. He carefully laid a fragile Christmas ball back in the tissue paper it had come out of. "I could be out filling my woodshed for next season."

That was not quite what she had meant by making the most of it! She had meant enjoying her and Jamie, but she couldn't very well say that.

So she said, "What I meant by making the most out of it was enjoying this tree and the kind of pioneer atmosphere up here."

He actually smiled slightly. "Consider me in the spirit, then. Pioneers worried about wood, believe me."

As she watched him go, it occurred to her it would not be a good idea to tangle with that particular tiger anyway.

Riley Keenan was way more man than a girl like her could handle.

She had made a mess of handling Sam, who had been a pudgy and rather unexciting real estate agent, nothing at all like that man who had just gone out the door.

She wondered, suddenly, what she had ever seen in Sam, and knew a jarring truth. She had not really seen anything in Sam. But she had always been the shy girl who lived in the shadow of her more beautiful and outgoing sister.

She'd been flattered when Sam asked her out, thrilled when he liked her. She had never even stopped to ask herself how she felt about him. It had been enough that he liked her.

But she had really begun to turn over a new leaf—to take charge of her own life—from the minute she had made that phone call to Mary Keenan about her cabin. A new Beth was emerging, bolder and more adventurous.

She wondered, with a shiver, what that might mean in terms of being stranded here in the wilderness with this incredible man.

If she was really in charge of her life, did it mean not succumbing to passing fancies, or did it mean exploring them? Oh, being the old Beth had been so much easier!

"Where are you going?" Jamie asked Riley worriedly.

"I'm going to chop some wood this afternoon."

"We have lots of wood," Jamie pointed out.

"You can never have enough wood in this country. I like to keep the woodshed topped up. It's a few cords short of full at the moment."

Jamie mulled this over. "Okay," he said. "I'll come help."

"No," Riley said firmly, "you stay and help your aunt with the tree."

"But—"

"Not this time," Riley said, and closed the door firmly behind him.

"Doesn't he like me?" Jamie asked sadly.

"Of course he likes you. His indifference is nothing personal." She sensed that was true, hoped it was true. Surely she could not find a man so wildly attractive who could be immune to the needs of her little nephew.

Another man, she reminded herself. The reason she had sworn off men. The problem with swearing off anything, was that the gods seemed to take it as a challenge. Swear off ice cream and the truck went by your house every day ringing its little bell. Swear off men, and you inevitably traveled thousands of miles into the isolated Canadian wilderness just to have one dropped on your doorstep.

And not just any old one, either. No, sir. The gods only taunted with the strongest, most virile, most attractive.

There was her answer. It meant not succumbing. And having Riley under the same roof was a test of her resolve, and she planned to pass.

"I so like helping him," Jamie said.

Future daddy in his inflection if not his actual words. She had to discourage him. "Jamie, he does not want your help."

She'd been too blunt. She saw that immediately. Discouraging was one thing. Shattering was quite another. "It's just that chopping wood is not a job small boys can help with. It can be very dangerous. I have some batteries for the tape player. Do you want to put on Molly Moffett's Merry Christmas while we finish decorating?"

The famous diversionary tactic.

"No," Jamie said. "We should save the batteries for Christmas Eve. Isn't that right, Buddy Bear?"

He manipulated Buddy Bear's head into a sage nod of agreement.

After an hour, she wished he and Buddy Bear would have gone for the diversionary tactic. To divert her. The steady sound of an ax thumping into wood somewhere out behind the cabin filled the afternoon.

The ice-cream truck passing once, you could say no to. But dozens of times? She was not made of steel, after all.

"We need the other box of decorations," she said, but they didn't really. What she really wanted was an excuse to go into the back bedroom and peep out the tiny window. Just one little look. Looking wasn't precisely the same as giving in to temptation.

The woodshed was in the trees behind the cabin. It was a three-sided building, the front of it open to the window she was looking out. It looked like it was overflowing with neatly stacked wood.

Riley was in front of it. The snow fell around him in huge featherlike flakes. He seemed as oblivious to the heavy snowfall as he had to the delights of the Christmas tree. He had a piece of wood on the chopping block.

She watched as he lifted the ax effortlessly, drew it up over his shoulder, then swung it with ease that was deceptive. The piece of wood on the block split clean.

With hardly a pause he stooped and put another one in its place.

She watched, embarrassed by her interest, annoyed at her lack of self-control, and yet inarguably mesmerized by the pure masculine power of this particular ballet.

"Did you find the decorations?" Jamie called.

She pulled back from the window and hastily found the box of decorations and brought them out into the main room.

But now she felt pulled to that window. It was pathetic, really. She pushed the desire to go back and look again aside. She succeeded for at least twenty minutes.

"I just need a sweater," she said. She stood at that back window, again, indulging in her guilty pleasure. Riley had taken his coat off, and was now standing in the swirling snow in his sweater, his breath coming out in frosty puffs.

She told herself a little entertainment was not unhealthy. She wouldn't feel guilty if she was watching an *E.R.* rerun just to see George Clooney. And they didn't have a TV here.

Despite how measured Riley's every move was, she wondered what drove him. He did not appear to tire out, and he did not miss. He chopped wood as if he were a machine, smooth, well-oiled, precise.

In fact, she realized, Riley Keenan chopped wood as if the devil was breathing down his neck.

She went back out to the tree. The room was too hot from the woodstove, and now she had put on a sweater! Despite her preoccupation, she was able to see the tree transforming, looking absolutely delightful. Not delightful enough to hold her full attention, though.

"I wonder if Buddy Bear needs a sweater," she said, and then felt guilty that she was going to use such a flimsy excuse to have another look out that window.

And even guiltier when Jamie nodded that Buddy Bear needed his sweater, apparently not noticing his aunt's profuse discomfort since she had put hers on. She made her way back to the bedroom, again and again, feeling as an alcoholic with a hidden bottle must feel.

Riley, unaware he was being watched, had slowly stripped off. It was the only sign he gave that he was in any way exerting himself. The sweater was gone, and he was out there in a long-sleeved shirt, the steam of his body heat rising wispily off his back.

She had to spend the night in the same cabin as

this man! She scurried back out to the tree, swearing off the vision out the window.

But Jamie was scrutinizing the tree carefully, and proclaimed it done. "I want to go play out in the snow, anyway," he said, "before it gets dark."

"All right. I'll come, too, for a little while before I start dinner."

They bundled up. She felt fat, in all her layers, and Jamie thought she looked hilarious, two good reasons to stay away from the back of the cabin and that woodshed. They went out into the crisp air. Her mission, she decided, was to stay in front of the cabin and out of Riley's way.

Out of sight, out of mind.

More evidence that whoever dreamed up these sayings knew nothing about the real world or real life.

For a while she was able to give herself over entirely to the joy of the snow. Jamie's last angels had almost disappeared under the wet blanket of new snow, so they made more. They made snow angels until she could hardly flap her arms anymore. And then they shuffled their feet and wrote their names in huge ten foot high letters in the snow.

"Let's go see what Riley's doing," Jamie said, sitting in the snow, eating white flakes off his mitt.

She decided that made it okay. That Jamie had suggested it. And besides, she looked fat and hilarious.

He was not going to see her as the kind of woman it would be dangerous to spend the night with.

Not that they were spending the night together, precisely. Not in the way most people would use that phrase.

"Auntie, how come your face is all red?"

"It's from the cold," she lied. "Yours is like that, too. Big red apples blooming on your cheeks."

Jamie led the way to the back of the cabin, and she went to great lengths to make it look like she was just being dragged along.

Riley was finally taking a breather. He was now down to a white T-shirt, even though the snow fell and melted on his naked arms. She could see the bulge of his biceps, pumped now from the exertion, and the strength in those forearms. The shirt was damp, and clung to the hard muscle of his breast and back, the flat hard line of his stomach.

He had the ax, head down on the chopping block, his wrists folded on top of the handle as he leaned on it.

His chest was heaving in and out, which made her very aware of the breadth of it, the power in his shoulders.

He heard them coming, and glanced up. As they got closer, she could see the job was not so easy as it had looked to be from the window. She could see the gleam of sweat on his face, his hair beginning to curl at the edges.

Casually he reached around and picked up his sweater. He wiped his forehead with it, then dropped it over his head, yanked it down around his chest.

"Gets cool when you stop working," he said, but she wondered if he had not seen the hunger burning in her eyes.

God, she was pathetic. If this afternoon had shown her nothing else, it had certainly shown her that. Pathetic. Powerless. Maybe being a take-charge kind of girl was not going to be in her nature.

It was a good thing she could always trust herself to be sensible. If he did not make the first move, she would be safe.

And looking at him, he was not a man who was going to make the first move. The gods were showing a little mercy after all.

There was split wood scattered everywhere around him, and he looked at it now, as if surprised. He swung the ax, and the gods must have had a little snicker at her reaction to how every line of his beautiful body was shown off in that split second. The blade sunk deep in the chopping block. He began to gather wood and move it toward the shed.

Without being asked, Jamie began to help.

She was out of place here. She saw that. And she knew she was susceptible to him. If he offered Jamie kindness now, as he had when they built the tree stand, she would be lost.

She did not even know what that meant, only that it would be dangerous, like swimming the English channel after only just getting your beginner's swimming badge.

"I have to go cook dinner," she said, and hoped it was not the strangled note in her voice that made him look up sharply.

He glanced at her, then at Jamie. "You go help your aunt."

"No. I'm helping you." This said as if they were fighting words.

Riley regarded his small champion for a moment, then shrugged and turned away. Jamie took this as *welcome aboard* and threw himself into his newfound position as a toter of wood.

Back in the cabin, Beth fought the demons inside herself. Part of her wanted to cook the best dinner Riley Keenan had ever eaten. Part of her wanted desperately to do that, to woo him, and to win him in the way that was so traditional to women.

But another part, wiser, recognized what that would be.

The beginning of the dance.

The you-man, me-woman dance, ageless. It was a dance, she reminded herself sourly, that she did not really know the steps to.

Instead of giving in to her desire to dance, she rustled through her suitcases until she found a novel she had brought. She read it into the fading light.

But when she heard Riley and Jamie's voices drifting nearer to the cabin, she looked at the book and realized she had not absorbed a single word. She would not know the protagonists' names if she was asked.

Still, determined not to let him see the slow melt happening inside of her, she got up off the couch, opened two tins of stew and put them on the stove.

When she saw Riley's face she suspected he had been driven in only by hunger. He looked tired. Snowflakes clung to his eyelashes, and drew her attention to the deep gray pools of his eyes. Something haunted resided there.

He glanced over her shoulder at the contents of the pot, and without a word, got a bowl down from a cupboard, and put flour in it. In seconds he had heated oil in a huge black frying pan and was frying his mix.

"What is that?" she asked, when the most heavenly smell began to fill the room, better even than the scent of the tree and the popcorn.

It was the smell of him.

"It's a fry bread," he said. "It'll go great with that stew. It's called bannock. I learned to make it from a Native friend, and the natives use it as a backwoods staple, but it's actually something the first Scots brought to Canada with them."

She glanced in his frying pan. The bread was

doubling up in size, and when he flipped it, it looked golden and delicious.

She exchanged looks with Jamie, who mouthed the words *he can cook*.

Which of course would move Riley a few notches up on the daddy-desirability scale since, aside from popcorn, and mini turkey once a year, Beth was no cook.

It could move him up her desirability scale, too, except she had banished it.

Still, it was almost too heady, standing shoulder to shoulder like this in this tiny kitchen, *sharing* the responsibility for getting supper cooked.

Sam's idea of having dinner together was she cooked, he channel-surfed.

The scariest thing of all was that this man beside her was nothing like Sam.

"Here," Riley said, "try a bite."

He was holding a piece of the hot bread out to her, and she leaned toward him, and nipped an edge off the bread.

It was hot and chewy, without a doubt one of the most delicious things she had ever tasted.

It suddenly seemed too intimate in the small kitchen. She felt as if she couldn't breathe, didn't know what to do with her eyes, had no words left in her.

She really didn't know if this was a dream or a

nightmare she was in. It seemed to her it had elements of both.

And that the gods were laughing.

Don't fight it, the voice inside her instructed. Go with it. Oh, she knew that voice. It had herded her into the bedroom all afternoon. It kept pointing out he was sexy. That voice was trying to take over from the more rational, sensible her.

She couldn't let it.

It wasn't just about her. It was about the child she was responsible for.

The only way she was not going to give in was to get away.

"I'm not feeling well," she blurted out. "I—I have to go lie down. Sorry."

Riley looked at her and then at the bread he had held out to her. "That bad?"

"No, it wasn't. It's not the bread." *It's you.* "Excuse me." And she bolted into her bedroom and shut the door. She lay on the bed and looked at the ceiling. She felt claustrophobic. She felt like she was in a prison cell. She felt like she had looked after herself, but failed Jamie.

Because he was still out there, falling in love. She could hear the rise and fall of their voices, the sounds of them doing the dishes together, Jamie talking Riley into playing a board game with him.

She'd deal with that part tomorrow. Tonight, she had just had to look after herself first, get her own head on straight first. She couldn't do that with Riley right there feeding her hot pan-fried bread.

Later, Jamie came in and threw his arms around her neck, gave her big sloppy kisses, none the worse for wear for his evening with Riley.

"There's a bed inside the couch in the living room," Jamie told her. "That's where Riley is going to sleep. I asked him to tell me a bedtime story, but he says he doesn't know any."

So he tucked in beside her, and she told him a bedtime story, and it gave the illusion that her world was safe and unchanged and the way it had always been.

But later, when she came awake with a start and the cabin was in pitch-darkness, she knew you could not cheat the gods, not outrun them, not hide from them.

The cabin was silent now, but somehow the deep, anguished cry that had awoken her still hung in the air.

A chill raced up and down her spine, and she felt goose bumps rise on her neck. Did she do the dangerous thing? Did she go to Riley and comfort him? Or did she do the safe thing and stay here and comfort herself?

What if there was no dangerous thing and no safe thing? What if there was only the decent thing? One human being who knew hurt, reaching out to another?

* * *

Riley made himself take deep steadying breaths. He listened. He was fairly certain he might have shouted in his sleep, the horror of the dream fresh in his mind. But he did not seem to have woken anyone else.

He had not had one of these dreams for a long time. He had dared to hope they were done. Now, as his eyes adjusted to the inky darkness of the room, he could see the Christmas tree outlined against the window.

That's when he'd known he was in trouble. When he'd foolishly agreed to help decorate the tree.

He had felt the darkness descending on him, then.

And made a decision to head outside, to work it out of his system. Oh, and he had worked. His hands were tough as leather, but he could feel the raw ache of blisters on both of them from the hold he'd had on that ax handle.

He'd come back here to the cabin, casting himself in the role of their protector. But he'd quickly seen what they needed protecting from was him.

From the dark shadow he could cast over their Christmas if he wasn't careful, if he didn't guard against the temptation to like the kid.

And her.

Bethany Cavell was not the remedy for a man with confused thoughts. *Her protector?* Oh, sure.

He could protect her from the porcupine, and he could keep the fire going, and he could make sure she didn't blow up the stove.

But he'd been aware of a larger issue as they had stood, side by side, cooking dinner.

He found her attractive. He liked her smell, and he liked the way she tilted her head, and he even liked the fact she was awkward around him, one moment shy, the next ready to do battle. He liked the soft huskiness of her voice, and the light that came on in her eyes when she looked at Jamie. He liked the way she tossed her hair, and the funny way she dressed, like a nun, being so careful not to show off those delectable curves that she possessed.

He did not think this was proper for a man sworn to protect. Still, he had given in to it just a touch. Lifted that hot bannock from the pan, offered her a bite.

Her teeth biting into it, her eyes on his.

And then the panic. He could swear she hadn't really gotten sick. She just knew. As he knew.

You couldn't put a man and a woman together like this without a little spark dancing in the air between them.

Why hadn't he thought of that back there on the road, when he'd had a choice of winching the truck out of the ditch or walking back here?

Oh, no, he'd had to try playing the hero one more time.

As if he didn't know what a miserable failure he was at that role.

A movement caught the corner of his eye, and he tilted his head. The white candy canes on her pajamas stood out in the faint moonlight.

"Riley?" she whispered.

So much for not having woken anybody up. "Yeah?" he growled.

"Is everything all right?"

"Yeah, fine. Go back to bed."

But she was not going back to bed. She was gliding across the floor toward him, being careful in the darkness.

"Did you have a bad dream?"

He closed his eyes, opened them again when he felt her weight settle on the edge of the pullout bed.

He was not a child. He was not Jamie. He did not want to be treated like Jamie. And most of all, he did not want her pity, her sympathy, her kindness.

"Yeah, I had a dream. Go back to bed. Sorry I woke you."

"I tried to go back to sleep," she said. "I couldn't. I thought if I had a hot milk it might help."

Hot milk. Other women might have suggested a nightcap. A reminder she was out of his league entirely. She was good and decent. As wholesome as whole wheat.

"Do you want one?"

"Sure." Now why did he say that? To get her off

the edge of his bed? Because he knew, once the dreams came, how hard it was to go back to sleep?

"Don't get up," she said, "I'll get it."

As if he was about to get up. He was in his underwear. He felt her get up, and instead of feeling relief, felt loss. A moment later the light flared to life in the kitchen, and he sat up on his elbow and watched her.

It was really unfair that he could watch her like this and she could not see him. He felt like a spy. And yet he could not look away from her.

It was as if she was an anchor of stability after the turbulence of that dream.

She was quite lovely. The pajamas were a bit too big. They swam around her delicate figure. Her hair was a mess, wild curls scattered every which way.

Alicia had always looked like hell when she woke up. Makeup all over the place, her mask off.

Bethany looked natural.

She began to hum. He thanked whatever gods had looked after him thus far that it was not a Christmas tune.

She poured steaming milk into mugs, hesitated, and then turned off the light, coming back to him through the darkness.

"It's harder to get back to sleep if you leave a light on," she whispered to him. He sat up and reached out his hand, and found the warmth of the mug, wrapped his hands around it.

"Thanks."

He thought she would take her milk and go to her room, but he felt her weight settle on the bed again. Foolish, but he shifted over, an invitation.

He didn't have a shirt on. His clothes, damp from being outside were hanging by the fire. He tucked the blanket in around himself.

She took the invitation, and they sat there in the darkness, looking at the tree, sipping the milk.

"I had insomnia," she said, "after my sister died. And nightmares."

"How did she die?"

"It was a car accident. She always drove really fast. She loved excitement. She died instantly. I guess that's something to be thankful for."

He wondered why people did this. In the grimmest of circumstances searched for something to be thankful for. For meaning.

What if there was nothing to be thankful for, and no meaning?

"What did you dream about?" she probed softly. "Maybe it would help to talk about it There was a friend I talked to lots after it happened."

"A boyfriend?" he asked, only partially to detour her from thinking he was going to talk about the dream.

She actually laughed. "No. No boyfriend. When I did have one it would have never occurred to me to talk to him about that."

He didn't know what it meant that he was happy about that, but he was sure whatever it meant, it wasn't good.

"Did you want to talk about the dream?" she asked, having missed the detour sign.

"I don't think so," he said, feeling some tension grow in him. He had thought what he least wanted was her kindness, and now he knew why.

It weakened him. It made him want to do the un-thinkable—to put his head on her shoulder, to feel her arms wrap around him, to let it out. To let it go.

She was silent for the longest time. He was not used to women who did not fill silences with the sound of their own voices.

He could feel his breathing moving into his belly, deep and relaxed.

"Do you dream about the fire?" she said, her voice a whisper. "The one you told Jamie and me about in the truck?"

He felt a band of tension return to his chest. He had told her he didn't want to talk about it. He was not going to answer her. She was prying. It was none of her business. It was no one's business but his own.

"Yes," he said, his voice rebelling against his command for silence. It was hardly a word, a croak, a whisper.

The silence embraced them again, deep.

And then he felt the touch of her fingers. Warm.

Soft. Gentle. She touched the scar, ran her fingers along where it started just below his ear.

He felt every muscle in his body tense up, and her fingers stopped moving, resting lightly, still, on the side of his neck, until he breathed again. When he began to breathe again, her fingers moved, tingling, down the column of his neck, over his shoulder, onto his chest.

He could feel something in the touch of her fingers on that damaged flesh. It was not revulsion, and it was not curiosity.

It was an exquisite tenderness.

It felt like it would penetrate that scar, and go to the wound unseen. The one in his heart. It felt as if there was something in her that could heal him.

If he let it.

Chapter 7

A noise, the smallest of rustles, awoke Riley.

He had no memory of going to sleep last night, nor any of her leaving him, though his senses told him she had. There was no weight on the other side of the bed, her soft, delicate scent was missing.

And yet, what lingered in his memory, as powerfully as if it was still there, was the softness of her fingertips on that scar.

He heard the rustle again, a faint breathless giggle.

He opened one eye cautiously.

And found himself looking into the beady glass eye of the stuffed bear.

"Hi," he said. It was morning, but he could tell by the weak, gray light coming in the window behind the Christmas tree, that it was early still, and that it was still snowing.

"It's the day before Christmas Eve," the bear announced, in a high, happy voice.

"Um." Riley said, not quite able to disguise his lack of enthusiasm. He closed his eyes and touched the scar on his neck, was almost surprised to find it was still there. The bear bumped against his face, and made a disgusting slurping sound.

Riley reminded himself the bear wasn't real, and so despite the sound, his cheek was as dry and clean as it had been a while ago. The bear was, in fact, attached to a little arm, and the arm was attached to something unseen, over the side of the bed, that giggled.

"Bears sleep in the winter," Riley said.

This was mulled over silently for a few seconds. "They wake up for Christmastime!" Jamie said, and then repeated it in his bear voice. "Yeah! We wake up for Christmastime."

Of course. Christmas. A time of magic for children and stuffed bears, the days counted down feverishly. Riley shifted over and looked over the edge of his bed at Jamie. Jamie was crouched on the floor, in flannel pajamas with—what else—bears all over them. He looked delighted to be discovered.

The child smiled at Riley, a genuine and joy-filled smile, as if having a crotchety cowboy as part of his morning was like having a dream come true.

Riley felt emotion closing his throat, completely unexpected. It was humbling that the kid kept giving him chances.

He wondered why it was that Jamie was so willing to give life more chances when it had dealt him such a lousy hand. He was five years old and he knew the loss of his mother, a loss that many people ten times his age had not yet experienced.

It occurred to Riley, looking into that face, shining with innocence, that he had a lesson to learn from Jamie Cavell.

The child had been wounded, but he was still willing to believe life was basically good. The child's very belief in Christmas, a season that symbolized miracles and hope and love meant he hadn't given up on life.

Riley had never put his own feelings about life into a precise statement before. But the truth was he had given up. Life had hurt him and he'd turned his back on it.

On Christmas Eve, six years ago, he had learned, the hard way, that he wasn't in control of everything. That there were things that all his strength and all his will and all his stubbornness could not hold back. If they had been small things, maybe he would have had a chance. But it had been a life and death thing where the force of his will had failed to bring the result he wanted. No, more than wanted. *Needed.*

And so what had he done? He had systematically made his world smaller and smaller so that at least he could be in control of that.

He saw now, with crystal clarity, that the shrinking of his world had only provided him with an illusion of control. A foolish illusion that he now saw could be shattered by something as small as a phone call from halfway around the world, a woman and a child looking for a cabin. A foolish illusion that could not even pass the test of a little snow.

So, again, he was brought to the most humbling of lessons. Men were not in control of the world.

As far as he could tell, they were not even in control of their own hearts.

Because, along with making his world small and controllable, he had tried desperately to turn his heart to a stone. It did not seem to be passing the test, either.

But Jamie seemed to know, already, that the world was an unpredictable place. He seemed to actually enjoy the fact he didn't know what was going to happen next. In fact, Jamie went forward, full bore, toward the very thing that had hurt him.

Did it take the purity of a child's heart to know that? The only thing that would heal anything was love.

Not science, not medicine, not psychology. Love.

How was it that a child knew you had to walk right back toward the very thing that had left you so wounded in the first place?

Jamie scrambled up on the bed beside him. "What are we going to do today?"

We. Yesterday, before gentle fingers had touched the scars on his neck, Riley would have divorced himself from that *we* as quickly as he could.

Beth had warned him about attachments after all.

But then Beth looked as if maybe she had as many trust problems as he did. She didn't look like she had all the answers.

Maybe in the spirit of the season, they should let the child lead them.

And if the kid was looking for a hero, if he wanted to get attached, was it that big a deal? Riley could send him postcards, maybe even send him a little present for his birthday, call him the odd time. Kind of like being a Big Brother, only from a comfortable distance.

If his aunt was close to the phone, he could say hi to her, too. As he thought about it, Riley thought it would be a great way to be a hero. From a distance. Pretty hard to spot the tarnish on the armor from several thousand miles away.

"What would *you* like to do today?" Riley asked.

"Well, to start I could make breakfast for Auntie, if you helped me. No one ever looks after her."

For a moment, Riley felt that emotion closing in his throat again. Because no one looked after Beth? Or because a little boy, who had just been asked what he'd like to do with his day, hadn't given one thought to himself. He'd thought about someone else.

"Cornflakes, it is," he teased.

Jamie shook his head. "No, that good bread you made for supper last night. And bacon. And eggs."

"She won't worry about getting fat?"

"My auntie? She never worries about that. Just about everything else."

A woman who didn't worry about getting fat. That was refreshing after Alicia who had counted calories feverishly, and lamented every drop of ice cream and square of chocolate that ever crossed her lips.

"She worries about everything else?" It was really unfair to pry information out of a kid, but somehow he didn't want to think of her fretting over every little thing.

He hoped it was something small. A dripping tap. A bothersome dog next door. Jamie arriving home five minutes late. If she had to have worries—and who didn't—those were the kinds of worries he wanted for her.

"She worries when the mail comes."

The mail? Hell. Bills.

"And when I go out to play."

What kind of neighborhood did they live in?

"She worries one of us will get hurt on the back stairs, cause they need to be fixed."

Riley was beginning to be ever so sorry he'd asked.

"I can fix them now, though, since you showed me how to nail yesterday." This was said with supreme confidence that quickly failed. "And after she thinks I'm asleep, sometimes she cries."

Hell, again. Those were not the kind of worries he wanted her to have.

"Don't worry," Jamie said. "I've got it looked after."

"You do, huh?"

"Me and Santa." He put a finger to his lips. "Shh. It's a secret."

Whatever she was worried about, she was going to have to stay worried about. Not much hope a five-year-old kid was going to be able to solve it. And Santa? Riley didn't want to be the one to break it to Jamie that Santa would be about as good at fixing things as Buddy Bear and the Easter Bunny.

"How about if you disappear for a few minutes, and let me get dressed." Not to mention try to wipe those distressing images Jamie had painted from his mind.

Bills. Broken stairs. Crying at night.

He dressed quickly, and looked out the window. The snow had formed a thick blanket of pure white quiet over everything. It hung heavy in the tree branches. And it was still falling, silent, heavy, from the sky. He could not see the mountains through the snow. Which meant the road would be a complete disaster by now.

"Still snowing," Jamie noted happily when Riley joined him in the kitchen.

Ah. Everything was a perception. For Jamie snow did not mean hazardous roads, it meant untold adventures.

For just one day, could he, Riley, drop the perception that the world was a place that hurt if you dropped your armor, if you made yourself vulnerable? For just one day, should he give himself over to what had been given to him? Without fighting it?

It sounded a lot like surrender.

There was no white flag in his arsenal of life-coping skills.

But maybe, just for today, Riley Keenan could let go of control, release his stranglehold on life and just see what happened.

He asked himself what he would do if he was completely free. If he wasn't trying to protect himself, and them, and if he wasn't in charge of the whole world.

And he looked into the small, eager face of Jamie Cavell and realized he wanted to give Jamie and Beth an experience with the Canadian wilderness that they would never forget. He couldn't take

Beth's worries away from her, but maybe he could keep them at bay for a few moments, a few hours, a few days.

He would follow Jamie's lead and think about what they might like to do and see. Carefree things. Snow things. Things they had not done before and would probably never do again. Today, he would show them the best parts of his world.

He smiled. And Jamie had already put in a request for bannock, definitely one of the best parts of his world. With Jamie standing on a chair beside him, he showed him the secret recipe for bannock and they made a platter full of it, to serve with syrup. Together they made bacon and eggs. When Jamie insisted on cracking the eggs, and broke every one of them, Riley reminded himself it was not about perfection but about perception.

"I love them scrambled," he said.

"Me, too!" Jamie agreed.

"You, too, what?" Beth came out of the bedroom. He saw again how fresh she looked in the morning, wholesome, with her hair messed, and the pattern of the sheet still pressed against her cheek.

He remembered her hand, the softness of her fingers.

His impulse was to escape, again, to the woodshed, to the mind-numbing monotony of pure physical work. He had to tamp it down. He had to remind himself, firmly, that he had decided to give life one day to teach him something, and he was not even fifteen minutes into that resolve.

So, instead of turning away from her, for once he did not try to hide what he was feeling. He smiled at her, tentatively, glad to see her, taken with her shy beauty. And she smiled back. Her smile was radiant, real.

And he didn't even try to pretend his heart didn't beat an extra beat inside his chest.

Some firmly held tension evaporated.

When breakfast was over, Jamie asked again, "What are we going to do today?"

"Have you ever made a snowman?" Riley asked.

"Never," Jamie said, shaking his head. "Could you really help me build a snowman? I've seen them in movies. Aunt Beth can give us a carrot to make a nose. I want a great big one!"

Riley laughed. "A snowman, it is."

Jamie sighed happily. "It will probably be in the *Guinness Book.*"

"Are you in?" Riley asked Beth. And he sensed they both knew the question was happening at two levels.

Was she in to build the snowman?

And was she in at a deeper level? No games and no guards? Was she willing to go where those cautious smiles promised to take them?

She hesitated. She looked at her feet, and played

with the bottom button on her pajamas, then twisted her hair around her fingers.

"Oh, no," she said, finally. "I'll do the dishes and straighten up."

"No, Auntie Beth, please. We might never see snow again."

"That's right," Riley said. "You might never walk this way again."

And again he knew he was talking about something different than snow. And she did, too. She looked at him, her smoky-green eyes wide and just a little bit frightened.

And then she ducked her head, and surrendered. "I'm in," she said.

"Yahoo," Jamie squealed. "Buddy Bear, isn't this the best Christmas ever? Isn't it?"

In that moment, Riley Keenan had never been so sure that he had done the right thing.

"Well, let's go," he said, "we're missing snow time."

Bundled up a few minutes later, he showed them how to make snowballs, then put them in the snow, and roll them. In this kind of sticky snow, the snow stuck to itself, and the balls just kept getting bigger.

"Like Velcro," Jamie said.

"Okay, you and your aunt against me," Riley said, after he had supervised the beginning of two substantial snowballs. "Let's see who can make the biggest one first."

It wasn't a fair competition at all. Even with Jamie's and Beth's weights and muscles combined, they would not be a match for him. He realized, a little sheepishly, that it was a form of male preening.

Not, thank God, that anybody else seemed to notice that. They were huffing and puffing and laughing, and the snowballs grew.

"I can't believe how heavy this is," Beth said.

"Don't hurt yourself," he advised her solemnly.

She gave him a dirty look, and she and Jamie leaned their weight back into it. Finally they could push it no more. Jamie peeked around it.

"Auntie, look!"

Riley liked auntie looking at him like that, all full of admiration for his great masculine strength. His snowball was huge, and finally it got to the stage where he could no longer push it.

"Come on, you guys. This is going to have to be a team thing."

They didn't need to be asked twice. Jamie and Beth came and joined him. Shoulders locked against the snow, legs braced and shoving, they pushed. Slipping and sliding and laughing, they put another layer of snow on the huge ball.

And then Beth's feet went out from under, and she made a wild grab, and knocked Riley off balance. Despite his efforts not to go over, he toppled right on top of her.

"Ouch," she said, but not very sincerely.

He lifted himself off her only enough that she did not have to take the full brunt of his weight. He could feel the quick rise and fall of her breast. His eyes locked on hers.

Hers were full of laughter, free of the worry and anxiety Jamie had told him she lived with daily in Arizona, free of whatever worries she had hauled along with her.

He had nothing to give them for Christmas, except this.

He reached out and touched her cheek, could not feel it through the glove, and so using his teeth he pulled the glove off and touched her cheek with his fingertips. He did not recall if he had ever touched anything so soft.

She went very still underneath him, the little puffs of steam coming out of her mouth stopped.

"Kiss her," Jamie crowed happily.

"Okay," he said, but at the last second he regained his senses, and he somehow managed to detour from the lips that beckoned.

He kissed her on the petal softness of her cheek.

And then he lifted himself off her, and got to his feet, put his glove back on and extended his hand to her.

She took it, and he pulled her up. She began to brush snow off herself, but not before he saw the look on her face.

She was disappointed.

Disappointed that he had not kissed her on the mouth. He suspected, at the same time, she had been terrified of it.

"Well, that makes two of us," he muttered.

"Two of us?" she asked.

"Soaked," he said. Then remembered his vow to be more real today. More vulnerable. "Terrified," he amended.

"Of what?" she demanded.

"Of you," he said.

"Oh, you are not. Why would you be afraid of me? I am not the kind of woman that men are afraid of."

"Maybe that's because men are generally fools," he said. "You're the type of woman they should be most afraid of."

She was blushing wildly. "I am?" she squeaked.

"Strong. Genuine. Real. And beautiful."

Her mouth fell open. She blushed even rosier. "I am not strong. Or beautiful. I'm just ordinary."

He felt a moment's anger at some unknown boyfriend who had not made her feel as beautiful as she was. And yet, if the boyfriend had done anything right, she would not be standing here.

And somehow, her standing here felt like the most right thing in the whole world, a blessing, a gift from the universe.

The thoughts were simply too intense, even for a

man who had taken a vow of absolute honesty. He scooped up a handful of snow and threw it at her.

She laughed, relieved, too, for a break from the intensity, and picked up snow and began shaping it into a careful ball.

And then he was running through the snow, with her chasing after him. He would let her get close and put on a little burst of speed and then let her get close again.

It was the little burst of speed that did him in. His foot skittered out from under him on an icy spot, and she tumbled right on top of him.

She rubbed her handful of snow gleefully in his face.

And then Jamie caught up to them, and Beth and Jamie were burying him in snow. He was laughing so hard he thought he would choke on snow. He tried, halfheartedly, to shake them off, making just enough effort to get Jamie shrieking with laughter and excitement.

He was laughing so hard his stomach ached and his jaw hurt.

He did not know when he had laughed like that before. Yes, he did. Never. He had never laughed like that in his entire life.

And then the laughter died, and they were right back where they had been before. At the place of that subtle electrical surge between a man and a woman, that place where the head turned off and nature kicked in.

Or was that the head turning off, and the heart being allowed to speak? Stone, crumbling.

"We better finish that snowman," Jamie said. "And then we can build a snowwoman and then a little snowboy."

Saved again.

But for how long? The little guy was going to have to sleep sometime. And Riley realized there was another dangerous hurdle coming right up.

He didn't have a change of clothes with him.

And he was soaked through to the skin.

The snowman was ridiculously large. It had taken all three of them as much effort as they could expend to get the middle ball of snow on top of the bottom one. The top ball "the head" Riley had to do by himself, using every ounce of his strength, while she stood back and blissfully admired. And not the snowman, either.

Jamie was circling it with the disposable camera she had gotten him at the airport. It was a beautiful snowman. Riley had gotten them two coals out of the stove for eyes, he had a humongous carrot nose, and smiling licorice lips.

On top of his head was Riley's cowboy hat.

Branch arms stuck out of his sides, and she and

Riley posed in his embrace. She was not sure when she had last had so much fun.

Not for a long, long time.

They went into the cabin, she sent Jamie to change and she put on soup for lunch. She tried not to look at Riley, but she was so aware of him. Especially now that she had felt the hard lines of his body on top of her own, especially now that she had felt the silk of his lips graze her cheek. Especially now that she knew he thought she was beautiful.

She shivered thinking about it, and then realized she was shivering because she was soaked and cold.

"You better go put on something dry," Riley suggested. He was already making fresh bannock to go with the soup.

She glanced at him, and saw the flesh on his arm was marbled with goose bumps.

"What about you?" she asked.

"I'm thinking on it," he said.

"You don't have any dry clothes stashed up here anywhere?"

"No, ma'am."

Ooh. The way he said ma'am, all soft and slow, was a dangerous thing.

"You better at least take that shirt off while you think on it."

He hesitated, only for a moment, and then slid the T-shirt off over his head, and went and hung it up to dry by the fire beside their coats and mittens.

She scurried into the bedroom and put on dry clothes, but when she came out he was as shirtless as he had been.

Save for the scar, which flowed down his chest like a lava pathway, he was simply too beautiful for words—all hard edges, and flowing lines, and taut muscle and unblemished skin.

Now she was standing in a kitchen cooking with a man with no shirt on, pretending it didn't fluster her in the least.

A beautiful man with no shirt on. She wanted to touch him. She wanted to finish the exploration that she had begun last night. She wanted to touch the hard mounds of his pectoral muscles, the taut flatness of his belly.

She noticed his face was whisker-roughened and that it made him look roguish and sexy and she wanted to touch his face, too.

Thankfully Jamie joined them before she was trembling from the effort of not touching.

"Are you cold?"

For a second she thought she had started trembling after all, and then she realized Jamie was talking to Riley.

"Nah," he said manfully.

"Yes, you are. You have goose pimples. It's because your jeans are wet."

"They'll dry."

Jamie frowned. "What if you get the hyperpottamus thing?"

"Hypothermia," he said. "I don't think you can get it standing inside a nice warm cabin sucking back soup."

"Jeans take forever to dry," she told him. "You should have told us you couldn't get wet."

"And miss all the fun?. I don't think so."

"No chance of hypothermia?" she asked, concerned.

"No. Don't worry so much. Today's your day not to worry about anything."

He said that as if he was giving it to her, a gift. But she couldn't let the man stand there and shiver.

"Auntie can make you something to wear. Right, Auntie?"

"Um—"

"Like the thing Hercules wears. You made me one out of a towel once," Jamie reminded her.

"A toga!" she said. "Out of a sheet. Or a blanket. That would work, wouldn't it?"

"Get real," Riley said, proud and stubborn. "I'm not wearing a toga!"

"It would only be for a little while," she said. "While we dried your stuff by the fire."

"No." But a little later, obviously very uncomfortable, he gave in. "I guess we could try it."

She found him a blanket and some safety pins,

and he disappeared into the back bedroom. He emerged a long time later.

"Don't laugh," he warned them.

Jamie stared at him. Then snickered.

"No laughing," he said. He had pinned part of the blanket over his shoulder.

His naked shoulder was quite incredible. So were his legs, strong, and straight, unbelievably muscled.

He marched past them, clutching the blanket around him. He made a beeline for the couch and sat down, pulled another blanket quickly onto his lap. He scowled furiously at them.

She tried to bite back the little gurgle of laughter at the back of her throat. It wouldn't cooperate.

Jamie chortled.

And then the three of them were laughing, the magic dancing in the air around them. While they waited for the jeans to dry, they drank hot chocolate and played Jamie's favorite board games.

When his clothes were finally nearly dry, he put them back on, and they all went outside and got wet again.

They built a mama snowman and a child snowman, and when they were done that they built a huge snow fort, with a door and a roof and tiny little peepholes. They flew a flag over it.

Beth felt like a child again.

The snow was magic. The day was magic.

But especially watching Riley was magic. It was

as if age and cynicism fell away from him. He was like a big kid, he gave himself over so completely to playing in the snow. He was wonderfully creative, awesomely strong, and with that combination he was able to bend the snow to whatever shape he demanded of it.

He was less shy at suppertime of taking off his clothes and donning the toga. He even pretended to be a Roman emperor as they played yet another hand of Go Fish.

And then, without warning, Jamie was asleep on the couch.

And she was alone with a man in a toga, with a fire burning in the stove, and the snow blowing outside.

Without warning she was a woman, and he was a man.

"I'll just go tuck him into bed," she said.

But Riley stooped and picked him up. She loved the strength of him, marveled at it, felt it stealing her breath from her throat, and her heart from her chest.

"Want to put his pajamas on?" he whispered.

"No, just pull off his socks and put him under the covers."

They laid him down together, stood side by side looking at him. She glanced up at Riley and saw the unguarded tenderness in his features. She knew that was where the real danger lay. Not in how strong he could be. Not in the beauty of his body.

The real danger lay in this part of himself that he mostly kept hidden.

They went back out to the other room, but now everything was changed.

It was awkward, like being on a first date. The toga made everything worse. Any other man would have looked so silly in it.

But he didn't. He looked like a man who would have fit in any age and any world. He could have been a warrior, an explorer, a hunter, a king.

"Well," she said, after a moment, "I should go to bed."

"You pulled that last night," he said.

"I did not. I was sick."

"No, you weren't. You were scared."

"Scared of what?" she demanded.

"Scared of me."

She wanted to deny it, but she couldn't.

"What if I told you I'm scared, too, Beth?"

"You already said that, but honestly, you don't strike me as the kind of man who is afraid of anything."

He smiled, but she sensed pain in the smile. "That was true, once. It's not anymore."

"What are you scared of?" she asked.

"The light in your eyes."

She gulped.

"And life," he said.

"Because of the fire," she guessed.

And he nodded. "Do you still want to hear about it?"

And she turned to him slowly, and knew that maybe she could have fought her attraction to his strength and his beauty, she could have fought the fact she was in a cozy cabin with a sinfully sexy half-dressed man.

But now he was offering her something else.

His heart, his soul, his most vulnerable places.

She would not be able to fight that. But she was also unable to say no. Instead she surrendered.

Chapter 8

"Do you want to pull out the couch into a bed?" he asked. "I could get rid of the outfit, then."

It seemed like it might be asking for trouble, but it also seemed like part of the surrender. It quickly became apparent he had the toga on his mind, not seduction, because he asked her to give him a minute.

She went into her bedroom and reviewed her surrender. It felt blissful after a day of fighting her growing awareness.

Beth was aware that all day, she had been experiencing a shift in the air, as if magic floated down around them in those feather-white flakes of snow.

Slowly some guard had let down in Riley Keenan. His laughter, deep and real, punctuated the day. She felt like a woman could live to hear his laughter. And he was playful, full of energy and mischief.

Unfortunately it made everything so much more complicated. Without the perpetual scowl, he was incredibly handsome, his face relaxed, his expression almost boyish. When he would turn, after smashing her with a snowball, and grin, he took her breath away. He was simply irresistible.

Jamie was blossoming under all that male attention. He had been glowing with happiness when they had tucked him in.

"Okay," he called.

She went back out into the main room. He was happily settled, the blankets drawn up under his arms, his back resting against the sofa back.

"I don't know how the Romans did it," he said.

But even the teasing note could not distract her from the fact now they were alone, and she could no longer deny the attraction. It was more than the detached interest of someone who appreciated great beauty.

There was something else there, right below the laughter, between her and Riley. A subtle crackle of electricity, a certain sexual tension.

He was probably naked under those blankets.

For God's sake, she told herself, he's naked under-neath his clothes all day, too.

And now, to complicate matters even further, Riley Keenan was handing her the most amazing gift. His trust. It was an unexpected and exhila-rating offering, like having a wild horse, majestic and untamable, suddenly turn toward you, stand its ground, then lower its head and come to you.

She stretched out on the bed beside him, on top of the blankets. She noticed the thick stubble of his whiskers and felt a naughty desire to feel their roughness against her cheek.

A treacherous voice inside her commented that she liked him in the toga better than under the blan-kets, but there was something about the way the covers draped over the large muscle of his thigh that made her mouth go dry.

"It was Christmas Eve," Riley said, and as soon as she heard the deep weariness in the tone of his voice, thoughts of togas and whiskers and muscu-lar thighs fled her.

Instead she watched the muscle in his jaw leap, as he forced himself to speak. "Five years ago. No, wait, six. My life had never been better. I had just bought the Rocky Ridge from my mom, who wanted to move into town. I'd been running the ranch since my dad died about six years previous to that. I was training horses, I was raising prize-winning beef cattle, I was about to marry the girl I'd dated since high school."

Don't ask something so silly, Beth ordered herself. But there was her voice, saying, "Was she pretty?"

Riley opened his eyes and looked at her. Really looked, as if he was seeing things she never saw herself when she looked in the mirror.

"She was very beautiful. She was told over and over again that she should be a model or an actress."

She felt herself flinch, but why would it surprise her that he would be with a beautiful woman? He was that kind of man. All women would love him. Why would he pick a little plain-Jane when he would have limitless choices? She had seen the women at the airport and the supermarket looking at him.

But she had also seen him look right through them, not interested.

"Alicia and I had been kind of wild kids," he went on, "Adrenaline junkies. Rodeos. Midnight drag races. Party until you drop. Then we decided to settle down. Not have kids or anything, but play grown-up. Build a house, run the ranch, raise cattle and horses. We were going to get married late in the spring."

Beth thought of that beautiful house they had passed on the way in. *He had built it for another woman.* Which was truly a ridiculous thought.

What did she think? He'd built it for her? Had a premonition of the future?

Ha. Even right this second he was not planning a future with Beth Cavell! She was pretty sure of that. And she was not planning one with him, either. She was just being uncharacteristically spontaneous.

Still, Beth did not think that his house had looked like a house where a wild woman who loved to party and drag race would live. It looked like a house that should be filled to the rafters with children, that should have a wading pool in the backyard, and a garden, and a pony tethered on the lawn.

Or was that her imagination? Superimposing some dream she had barely acknowledged for herself onto his life?

"Alicia and I had been at a Christmas Eve party in Calgary and we were heading back out to my place. We were on that stretch of highway between Bragg Creek and my turnoff. Back off the highway, down a long driveway up on a hill was an old mobile home. When we passed it something made me look over. I drove on by, but I'd seen a flicker of light inside the living room window. At first I didn't think much of it, but it kept bugging me, and a half mile or so later I still couldn't get it out of my mind, so I turned around and went back. Alicia was cranky about that. She had some last-minute Christmas wrapping to do—that was Alicia—and she wanted to get home."

Hallelujah! Alicia-the-beautiful had been cranky. Oh, God. They had lived together.

"She lived about twenty minutes past my place."

No, they hadn't lived together! This was craziness. Of course he had a history. And it was unbelievable she would react emotionally to it.

What was happening to her? What had the day playing in the snow done to her sensibilities?

"By the time I pulled back into that driveway, I couldn't believe it. The inside of that living-room window looked like a pumpkin, glowing orange. The trailer was on fire. I told Alicia to use her cell to call it in, and I put the pedal to the metal. I must have gone up that driveway at a hundred and ten miles an hour. Up close, out of the vehicle, I could see in the living-room window. The Christmas tree was on fire. The whole front room was on fire."

Beth was aware that a shift happened in her, right then. She became less tuned in to herself and much more tuned in to him. His voice was raspy with pain. He hated talking about this.

"Then I noticed there were toys all over the front yard, and I figured there might be kids in there. It sounds slow when I tell it, but my mind was going at warp speed. Like by the time I had that thought about the kids, I was already kicking down the front door. In the background I could hear Alicia screaming at me to stay out, begging me to stay out, not to be such an idiot, to be safe, telling me to let the fire department look after it.

"But I knew the fire department was a long way from coming. I could not believe the heat and the smoke that hit me when I went through the door. There was this eerie glow coming from the living room, but everything else was really dark and disorienting. It was hard to breathe, and it was heat like I had never experienced it before.

"I pulled my shirt up over my face, and crouched down and went down the hall to the first door. It was a bedroom. There was a woman, and I woke her up. I busted out the bedroom window and just dropped her out of it. She was half asleep and terrified. She screamed at me to get the kids, that they were in the bedroom next to hers.

"I found the bedroom. The door hadn't been shut so it was really dark and smoky. I was reaching out in front of me trying to see if there was anything in there. And there were two little kids, sleeping together in this double bed. I scooped them up, one under each arm like footballs, and got the hell out of there.

"I got outside, and put the kids down and they ran to their mama, and I had blood all over my arms from smashing the window, and it felt like my lungs must be singed black. I couldn't stop coughing, but even bent over double from it I noticed the air tasted good. I felt like I had never fully appreciated what it was to be alive before. I noticed people were showing up now. The flames were shooting right out the ceiling and people were coming from miles around. I could hear sirens in the distance.

"And then I heard someone screaming a child's name. Ben. Over and over.

"I turned and looked, and it was the woman I'd tossed out the bedroom window. She had both those kids in her arms, but this wild-eyed tormented look on her face. And then I realized there was another baby in there."

He stopped. Beth could feel the faintest tremble of his big frame, so she moved very close and took his hand. Her own thoughts were now completely turned off, and she was totally focused on him.

The skin on his hand was rough, and despite the tremor, his grip was one of unbelievable strength. She was not sure anything had ever felt so right as his hand in hers.

"I headed back in. Alicia grabbed me. She tried to hold me, she was holding on like a wildcat, and sobbing hysterically, but I broke her grip on me, and pushed her away. Another guy tried to grab me, too, and I was even less nice to him. And then I was back in there.

"It was an inferno. I felt like my skin was melting. I called out the kid's name, Ben, but my voice just got sucked into the roar of the fire. I started to go back down the hall, trying to think. Would the other baby be in the same room as the other kids had been? Did I even know which room that was anymore? It was so weird in there, like hell."

His voice broke, and he was silent for so long she thought maybe he had decided not to tell the rest.

She held his hand, accepting.

He took a deep shuddering breath, and his voice was very soft. "I didn't get very far. Part of the roof collapsed on top of me. The next thing I remembered I was in the hospital being treated for burns and smoke inhalation." His lips twisted into a pained smile that held no amusement. "I was being heralded as a hero."

She did not want to ask. She knew the answer already. And yet her soul knew that he needed to tell it all, he needed to purge himself of every last painful detail.

"And the other baby?" she whispered.

Silence, and then Riley drew in a steadying breath. "He was two. They found him curled up underneath the bed, hiding. Nobody knows why he was under there. He—" Riley marshaled his strength "—didn't make it."

"Oh, Riley. Oh, Riley." The tears came of their own accord, washing down her cheeks. She made no attempt to brush them away.

"Yeah. Some hero, huh?"

She was very, very quiet. She knew it did not matter what words she tried to say, she could not take this pain away from him. It would not help to remind him three people had lived because of him. He already knew that, and it had not helped him.

"Tell me the rest," she finally said softly.

He glanced at her, briefly, surprised. "Most people would say that was the end of the story."

"Tell me the rest," she said again, knowing it was not the end of the story at all, knowing this was the reason for the aloofness in his eyes, for the way he stood apart, for the reason he had gone to chop wood instead of decorating the Christmas tree.

He sighed. "The rest. I couldn't stand the hero stuff. I literally could not bear it. Papers wanted interviews. The local news sent cameramen out to the ranch. I stopped answering the phone and opening the door. That died down and then I was awarded some medal for bravery. The day I was supposed to get it I was so far back in the hills on my horse they couldn't even find me. That's when I found out I liked it back there. I liked going back into the hills for days, just being by myself with my horse and some cows."

Beth had a feeling of understanding him perfectly, of knowing exactly why he would do that, why he craved solitude. She could feel her heart swelling in her chest, almost as if loving him would be too big to hold.

Loving him. How could she love him? She barely knew him. But at this moment in time, it felt like the whole universe had conspired to bring her to this man. And her love for him felt so pure. And so simple. Of course she knew him. You did not hear a story like that and not know the person who had told it.

She remembered looking at those scars the first night she'd seen him, and thinking, in a way she had not yet understood, they were a part of him.

Now she understood the scars represented, perfectly, his raw and undiluted brand of courage.

"I think you're a hero," she said, finally, "whether you want to be or not." She knew he was her hero, whether she ever told him or not.

Riley shook his head, looked at the ceiling. "You see, Beth, to be a hero, you have to make a choice. And I have to tell you something I've never told anyone else. I never made one single choice from the moment I spotted that first flicker of light. It was like I was operating on some instinct so deep inside of me that my brain wasn't even turned on. I didn't *decide* to go into the fire. I just went.

"When people tell me I was courageous, I want to laugh. In order to be courageous you have to be afraid. I wasn't afraid. I was operating like an animal, on some gut instinct that went beyond my mind, my fear, my control.

"Alicia never got that. I don't think she ever forgave me for not listening to her that night. Sometimes, I'd see her looking at the scars, just a quick glance, and I could feel her anger and resentment. Her revulsion. It was as if she felt I deliberately plotted to ruin our lives."

"Ruin your lives?"

"Our relationship didn't work. It just slid downhill after that. It wasn't her fault. I was different. Before that I'd been an ambitious young guy who liked to have a good time. She did, too. I was going to make a zillion dollars raising cutting horses and cattle, she was going to spend it. I was going to expand my spread, and we were going to travel the world showing horses and making big cattle deals and generally being big shots.

"But after that Christmas Eve, nothing mattered to me anymore. Those kind of dreams seemed downright dumb. I couldn't handle being around people. Parties made me sick to my stomach. Nothing gave me a rush, not driving too fast, not riding bulls, nothing. I didn't feel like making money was important. I felt like the Rocky Ridge just the way it was, was enough. I didn't want to see the world. Even after all that hero garbage finally died, I couldn't feel the same anymore. My whole life up until the point of that fire seemed like it had been superficial and unreal and ridiculous.

"Alicia hung in for a couple of months but she wanted things to be the same as they were before, and I already knew that was never going to happen. One day, she told me I just wasn't fun anymore and gave me back the ring. It was true. I didn't have any interest in having fun, or being fun. Somedays it felt like I was lucky to be able to put one foot in front of the other.

"Fun? How could I have fun when I wanted to know why I got to live, and that child had to die? What had I ever done with my life that made me worthy of living? All the chances I took, and death never grabbed me. But that baby had his whole life ahead of him. A fresh slate. He didn't get a chance.

"I'd spend days chewing over what I should have done differently. I should have stopped when I first saw the flicker of light, instead of thinking on it. Those few seconds might have made the difference.

"I should have never assumed I had them all on the first sweep through the trailer. I wondered if it was me breaking the window to put his Mom outside that made the little guy hide under the bed."

A steady darkness was falling on the cabin. Beth looked at his chiseled features in the fading light.

"The mom sends me a Christmas card every year. With pictures of the other two kids. Sarah and Daniel. She never mentions Ben. She never held it against me. She never blamed me. Nobody did. But I can't stop blaming myself. I don't guess I ever will, now.

"And that," he said slowly, "is why I hate Christmas."

Darkness fell completely around them. She said

nothing for the longest time, and then she said, "I'm glad you didn't marry her, Riley."

"Huh?"

"Alicia. It's good you didn't marry her." Beth was aware the words were not coming from a place of her own self-interest at all. "I don't believe she left you because the fire had made you not fun anymore. It was that it was taking you places that she couldn't ever go. It was showing you the depths of your soul. She never knew who you were, Riley. She would have never tried to hold you back from going into that fire if she knew."

"You really believe that?" he asked softly.

"I know it."

"I don't think of her much. When I do, it feels like we were strangers." He glanced at her, smiled, his smile tired. "How could someone so young and pretty as you know anything about the depths of souls?" he asked.

She registered that he thought she was pretty, even while she thought carefully about her answer.

Finally she said, "My sister's death stripped away every veneer I had, and I am, ever so slowly, finding out who I am and who I am not."

"And?"

She laughed softly. "And some days are better than others. I always thought I wasn't good enough, and then I found out I was good enough for Jamie.

How much better than that could any person ever want to be?

"I found out I wasn't a girl, I was a woman. But some days I still feel like I don't know exactly what that means, or who I am. Am I strong or weak? Is there any of my sister's fire in me? Did she do everything right, and did I do everything wrong, or are there parts of both of us that were good, and parts of both of us that were not so good?"

"Tough questions," he agreed, and she was so grateful that he did not try to shed any light on them. "By the way, Jamie told me about the old boyfriend. Said he left you because of him."

"Jamie knows it was because of him?" she asked horrified.

"Yeah. Nothing personal. But he sounds like he was a jerk."

"Nothing personal, but Alicia doesn't sound like she was any prize, either."

They laughed softly over that.

"When my sister died," she said, "I realized life was trying to tell me something, and I wasn't listening. It got my attention."

"The hard way," he said bitterly.

"Sometimes that seems to be how it works, Riley, the hard way."

"Sorry. I'm having trouble seeing what life was trying to tell me that night."

"Is it possible life was trying to show you who you were?"

He snorted. "A grumpy reclusive cowboy?"

It was her turn to snort. "You are a man of incredible strength and depth, a man with such an enormous soul it would not allow you to be devoured by the life you were planning for yourself. You are a man of sensitivity and power, and that is a rare combination."

"Beth, you really don't know that much about me."

She smiled in the darkness. "Yes, I do," she said. "I know a great deal about you. I know you have wandered in the wilderness, and you are trying to find your way home."

He was silent.

"Do you know the way home?" she whispered.

"No," he whispered back.

She leaned over and touched his whisker-roughened cheek with her lips. "Me, either," she said. "I think we can find the way together."

Her lips slid over, and shyly touched his. And when he answered, the shyness evaporated, and boldness took its place.

Suddenly she felt like she knew who she really was after all.

Her lips touched his, sweet as spring water.

And when he accepted what was in that sweet

kiss—acceptance, forgiveness, serenity—he knew something very important had just happened.

He had been running for six years.

And this sweet woman beside him had somehow convinced him to turn around and face his demons, head-on. To look them square in the eye.

He was surprised to find the demons had shrunk and so had he.

He saw himself in a new light. Not as a big, powerful man who should have been able to change the events of that night, but as just an ordinary man who had found himself in extraordinary circumstances and done his best.

His very best. He had held nothing back. He had been willing to sacrifice his own life. His sacrifice had been refused.

Not refused because it wasn't good enough, or he wasn't good enough. Refused kindly. By a universe that had protected him, though he had not acknowledged it until now.

But had not the last six years been good years? Aside from the fact he had chosen a lonely existence, had he not really discovered who he was?

A simple man, without grandiosity. A hardworking man, easily satisfied with what he had. A man who had tried to find himself in good times, in a beautiful woman, in things, in collecting stuff and who had, in the end, been given the gift of seeing how empty all that was.

Somehow, over the past six years he had become the most amazing thing.

A good man.

A man who would not let a woman and child get snowed in in strange territory. Six years ago, he would have just said, tough, they made the decision, let them live with it.

But that fire had pushed a whole other side of him to the forefront. A man who was willing to give something back to the world, to make sacrifices for others.

And once that man had been released, he was never creeping back into the shadows again. He understood that's what had driven Alicia away. He had changed in some fundamental way that made them completely incompatible.

The scars he bore on his neck had reminded her of that every single day. That he was changed, new, and she was not.

Six years he had spent, trying to come to terms with who he now was.

Was it a coincidence that the answer should come to him, in the very season that he had first begun his trek through the wilderness. He realized there was one step left, before his journey was done.

He needed to forgive himself.

Her questing lips were chasing all thought from him.

He was filling with the deepest sense of contentment. He accepted the invitation of her lips.

Felt the atmosphere change between them, become bold and heated.

He had never wanted anyone the way he wanted her. She was fresh and real, tried by the fires of life, just as he had been.

And she, too, had emerged strong. A good woman, and a decent one.

He felt the softness of her skin, ran his hand along the silk of her arm, and shoulder, lifted her hair to feel the tender flesh at the back of her neck.

He took his mouth off of hers, and kissed along the trail that his hand had blazed. He kissed her arm, and pulled her T-shirt down off the creamy swell of her shoulder and kissed that. He kissed the sweet curve of her neck, and the lobes of her ears.

She sighed beneath his kisses.

It was that sigh—of happiness, of contentment, of bliss—that brought him to his senses. The man he had been six years ago, would have taken whatever she offered. Taken it, and not asked one single question about tomorrow.

But the man he was now knew he had to live with himself.

And knew he had to live with the new reality. That he was a good man, and a decent man.

And that he had come to this cabin to protect this woman and her child.

They were leaving. He was staying.

Beth Cavell was not the kind of woman who could take something like making love lightly, even if she convinced herself of that in the heat of the moment.

He realized he had been running from the label of hero for a lot of years.

But that's what he wanted to be right now.

And maybe, in the end, that was what made men heroes, or not. Not whether they raced into burning buildings and saved children.

But the kind of everyday decisions they made. Did they act with complete integrity at all times? Was their strength more than physical? Could they do the day-to-day things in a way that honored the spirit that burned so bright and sacred within them and around them?

He wanted, more than he had ever wanted anything, to be Beth Cavell's hero. And so, though it caused him pain, he lifted her T-shirt back over her shoulder. He kissed her lightly one more time, on the forehead.

"Don't stop," she begged.

Ah. So heroes were tested.

Because he didn't want to stop. Oh, God, he

wanted to kiss her until neither of them could breathe, until both of them trembled with weakness and wanting. He wanted to take off her clothes, slowly, unveil the delights of her, and braille every inch of her with his fingertips and then his lips.

He wanted to feel her lips on his face, and to feel her hands, shy, undoing the brass snap on his jeans.

"We have to stop," he said.

"Why?"

"Because you aren't this kind of girl."

"Yes, I am."

He actually laughed, held her close to him so that she would not feel stung, rejected. He wanted her to understand it wasn't out of unkindness he was stopping this.

No, the exact opposite.

It was an act of love.

The purest love he had ever known. It was an act of putting her needs ahead of his own. And she did not need a one-night stand with a cowboy whom destiny had dumped on her doorstep.

He knew he had made the right decision, because he felt her relax against him, not nearly as ready to take that gigantic step as she had wanted him to believe.

After a while he felt her breathing grow deep and steady, and marveled at the tenderness he felt at her slight form pressed into his, her breath warm against his shirt, her hair falling across his arm.

But he did not sleep for a long time, though he felt exhausted. More exhausted than he felt after a day of breaking colts or branding cattle.

A deep, good exhaustion.

Maybe it was because he was so exhausted that he was nearly asleep before it occurred to him, he had used the word love, in his own mind, to define how he felt about her.

It was impossible, of course.

He barely knew her.

And yet, he felt the strangest sense of having always known her.

Something very un-hero-like leaped in his breast. He recognized it immediately. It was terror, plain and simple.

He slipped his arm out from underneath her, and folded it underneath his head. He stared at the ceiling, sleep chased away, though the exhaustion remained.

Should he go? He could probably get his truck out of the ditch and plow his way home by morning.

But what had changed? He still was not in a position where he would be comfortable leaving this woman and child here by themselves. It was still snowing. Untold dangers still lurked. Or had all that just been an excuse?

Had he seen his own healing in the depths of her eyes from the first moment?

Riley Keenan was used to being lonely. He was

used to being irritable. He was used to handling life on his own terms.

What he was not used to, was a feeling of not knowing what to do. He had always been decisive, a man of complete action.

Go or stay? He fell asleep still wrestling with that question.

"It's the morning of Christmas Eve," a high, excited voice told him.

Riley opened one eye and looked at the bear. A little hand around its neck was making it dance, to and fro. So he had stayed. Somehow he had made a decision without making one at all.

He became aware of softness, a sweet weight pressed against him.

Jamie peeped up over the side of the sofa bed. His eyes widened. "Is that Auntie Mommy?"

"Um."

"It is Auntie Mommy!"

"So it is," Riley said, feigning surprise.

"Did you sleep together?"

Not in the way that question usually implies. "Kind of."

Jamie nodded sagely. "Were you scared last night?"

Terrified. "Why do you ask?"

"Auntie Mommy comes and sleeps with me if I'm scared, too."

Riley realized he was face-to-face with incredible innocence. Jamie had no idea a man and a woman sleeping together had connotations. The child had not had men in his life. Auntie Mommy's old boyfriend had not stayed overnight.

Why did he feel so good about that? Possessive? Fiercely so?

"Let's make Auntie Mommy breakfast again," Jamie said, and then leaned very close. "And then I would like you to take me sledding. Just you and me. And Buddy Bear would like to come." He paused and lowered his voice to a whisper. "I have to tell you a secret."

A hero would be worthy of a little boy's secrets.

Chapter 9

"Auntie Mommy, after breakfast, Riley and Buddy Bear and I are going sledding. Just the guys."

Beth looked up from her breakfast, startled. She was positively glowing this morning. Riley was not sure he had ever seen a woman look so beautiful.

No, she was not Alicia's kind of beauty. No mask came off at night. There was nothing polished about her.

She had been right about one thing last night: He had narrowly escaped making the worst mistake of his life.

"You are not going sledding without me," she said, miffed.

"Just guys!" Jamie insisted.

"No. There is no such thing as just guys. Your mother and I did not raise you to be a miniature sexist."

Jamie frowned. "What's a sexist? Does that have to do with sex? Because Bobby Dunlop was telling me all about that and Mrs. Beckett, my teacher, said he's not allowed to, that we don't discuss sex in kindergarten."

Riley tried not to laugh at the disapproving look that Jamie was leveling at his aunt.

"Bobby Dunlop was telling you about sex?" she asked. "What did he say?"

"I just told you, I'm not allowed to tell you while I'm in kindergarten. Maybe in grade one. I'll ask."

"You're allowed to tell me! You're allowed to tell me anything."

"Are you sure?"

"Of course I'm sure."

"Well, don't tell Mrs. Beckett I told you, just in case."

"Cross my heart."

Riley liked this little interaction immensely. Beth may have been thrust into motherhood before she felt she was ready, but he saw that she was born to it. He saw the answers to each of those questions she had asked about herself last night were evident in this interchange.

She *was* good enough. And she was stronger

than she thought. Her fire, not her sister's, lurked right underneath the gentleness of those silver-green eyes. She probably did do things wrong, but he would have bet his life that she did many more things right.

"Well, Bobby got guinea pigs," Jamie explained. "Two. They were supposed to be boys, but one wasn't. One was a girl. It takes a boy and a girl. Sex does."

"Okay," Beth said, and Riley could see she was nibbling her lip to keep from laughing, "I'm with you so far."

"So then they were in the same place together and they had babies. Can I have one? I was going to ask for Christmas but I forgot when you told me I was coming to Canada."

"No guinea pig. No pets."

Riley suddenly wasn't enjoying this quite as much. "No pets?"

"We live in a trailer park," Beth explained, "that's one of the rules. No pets."

He did not like thinking of Jamie growing up with a rule like that. Growing boys needed pets. Real pets, too, not guinea pigs. A growing boy needed a good dog. And a place he could keep the snakes he found. By the time he was ten, Riley had had his own dog, his own horse, and his own twenty-two rifle.

He did not like to think of them being in a trailer, either. "A newer model, right?" he asked.

"Pets?" she asked, baffled.

"Trailer," he said.

Understanding dawned in her face, it softened with the most exquisite tenderness. For him and for the pain he had been through.

It made him feel like his chest was wide-open and she was seeing the very beat of his heart. It was not a sensation he enjoyed. "I think we need to get back to the sexist thing," he said.

"A newer model sexist?" Jamie asked, baffled. "Or pet?"

"The trailer's three years old," she told Riley. "Perfectly safe. And Jamie, a sexist is a man who thinks women shouldn't do certain things. For instance, he might think a woman shouldn't have a job driving a truck."

"But a sexist could also be a woman who didn't think a man should be a nurse," Riley pointed out helpfully.

"He's only five. Don't confuse him. The point I am trying to make is it offends me that I'm being excluded from tobogganing because I'm female."

Jamie pondered that. "Okay," he decided. "You can't come because you have light-brown hair. Me and Riley and Buddy have dark hair. Just the dark-haired people."

"Now we're going to talk about prejudice," she said.

Riley suddenly saw, very clearly, why families should have a man and a woman. For as good a mother as Beth was, she had this distressing tendency to explain everything, to turn everything into an opportunity to teach. Sometimes a kid just needed a boss.

"Your aunt's coming with us," Riley said. "No discussion."

"Oh. Okay. I can tell you later."

"Tell him what later?" Beth asked suspiciously.

At the distressed expression on Jamie's face, Riley said, deadpan, "Oh, it's guy stuff."

She threw up her hands and made a face, and Jamie scrambled into her lap and kissed her on the cheek.

"It doesn't mean we don't love you, Auntie!"

We. Really, a correction was in order, but somehow Riley couldn't work up any enthusiasm about making it.

She smiled. "Now that's what I needed to know!"

There was a great hill for sledding not far from the cabin. Riley remembered coming here when he was a boy with his father. They would come to get firewood, but the sled was always in the back of the truck.

In moments, he was revisiting those joyous carefree days.

He dragged the sled halfway up the hill, with Beth and Jamie trailing behind him. They were all panting from exertion. The snow still fell.

He supervised the loading. Jamie first, Beth next, him last, his arms wrapped around her waist, his chin tucked into her shoulder.

She screamed all the way down the hill. Jamie laughed.

After two times, Jamie was exhausted, and Riley put him on the sled and pulled him up.

"All the way to the top, this time," Beth said.

He slid her a look. It was a good thing he hadn't left her up here at the cabin on her own, after all.

"Under the sweet librarian exterior, I see you have a secret daredevil side," he said.

"Librarian?" she gasped, wounded. "Is that how you see me?"

"When you're in grade one," he told her, "I'll tell you how men feel about librarians."

"But I'll never be in grade one again!"

He shrugged. "Too bad, then."

He had to race to the top of the hill to avoid being smacked by her. Then they sailed down, at breakneck speed. The sled dumped them in a heap at the bottom, and they fell on top of each other, laughing.

"I thought I was in pretty good shape," he said by the tenth or eleventh run, "but this is killing me."

Of course, nothing was further from the truth. It had been a long, long time since he had been so happy. It wasn't killing him at all. In fact, unless he was mistaken, for the first time in a very long time, he was saying a resounding yes to life.

She looked at her watch. "It's lunchtime. I guess, since I'm stuck with sexists, I'll have to go make it."

"I'll do it if you want," he said easily.

"No. Go ahead and have your guy time." She sat down on the hill and slid down on her pants, hooting the whole way.

Riley sat and watched her go. He looked at the mountains, and the snow, breathed deeply the clean good air.

This was really the life a small boy should have. Maybe they could come back in the summer. Maybe he could send them a ticket.

Jamie trudged back up the hill, Buddy Bear riding the sled.

"This is the most fun I've ever had," he said. "Ever. Even better than lazar tag at Bobby's birthday last year."

The little boy sat down beside him, then realized he didn't have Buddy Bear. He carefully retrieved him from the sled, and put him on his lap.

"I wanted to tell you a secret," he said.

"Okay."

"If I tell you what I asked Santa for for Christmas, will I still get it?"

Riley felt he was a man with too many rough edges to be trusted with such a delicate question.

"I don't know," he said, deciding for honesty. "I'm not much of an expert on Santa."

"You were a kid once, weren't you?"

"Yeah. A long time ago. I've almost forgotten."

"Don't be silly. You don't forget things like that. Did Santa always bring you what you asked for?"

Another tough question. "No," he said, finally, deciding on honesty again.

"He didn't?" Jamie sounded panicky.

"No, he didn't. But he always brought me what I needed."

Jamie pondered that for a minute. "What's the difference?"

"Well, like I might have wanted bullets for my twenty-two rifle but I might have needed mittens."

The boy did not look reassured by that. "What I want and need are the very same thing."

"Well, then—"

"It's actually not for me. I asked for something for Auntie Beth."

"You asked Santa for something for your aunt, instead of yourself?"

He nodded vigorously. "You see, she worries all the time. And she can't do anything. I told you about the broken stair. And she looks sick when the bills come in. And when she thinks I'm sleeping she cries. And Sam left her because he didn't want me."

"And how did you figure Santa could fix all that?"

"That's the secret." Jamie paused and then said with great relish, "I asked him to bring me a daddy."

Riley couldn't trust himself to speak. He felt like he'd been hit in the stomach with a sledgehammer. "You did, huh?" he finally said weakly.

"Yup."

He tried to think carefully before he spoke. "You know, Jamie, I think Santa can do mittens and toy trucks and bikes and stuff like that. I don't think he has any people in that red sack of his. I've never heard of that."

"You haven't?"

"No, never."

"Well," Jamie said stubbornly, "I think he just delivers the people early. I figured that out already."

"When did you figure that out?"

"At the airport."

Great. This was the biggest mess he'd ever been in. Jamie thought he was the Christmas daddy Santa had delivered. Somehow it was all her fault. She should have warned him.

Something tickled his memory. Hadn't she tried to tell him something? She'd told him Jamie was looking for a hero. That was a hell of a long way from a dad.

A hell of a long way.

And that's what he planned to tell her. As soon as he calmed down enough to say it without inserting two dozen swear words in the sentence.

* * *

Beth heard them come in the door. So this was how love felt. Your heart raced at the sound of a certain footfall on the step.

Just as she could see how lucky he had been not to marry Alicia, she saw, suddenly how lucky she had been not to follow through with her plans for a future with Sam.

She had not loved him. At some point she had decided love was the stuff of fairy tales, and she'd been prepared to settle for what she'd found with Sam.

Now, in the first throes of love, she didn't know what to do when Riley came in the room. Did she let this feeling show on her face? Or would that be too pathetic?

What would Penny do?

Penny would race over to him and hug him and kiss him silly.

Well, she couldn't quite be that much a Penny, but she could meet halfway between what Beth would usually do, and what Penny would do.

She wiped her hands on the dish towel and went to greet them.

Her smile faded. The thumping of her heart stilled. What was wrong?

All the warmth was gone from Riley's face. All the tenderness. All the easy laughter. This was not the man who had held her last night, who had cooked her breakfast, who had held her on the toboggan, who had taken her hand going up that hill, who had teased her and made her laugh, and made the sun come out in a world that had all gone gray.

This was the man who had met them at the airport.

No, worse, because that man had only been impatient. And there was no doubt that this one was more than impatient.

He was angry. It showed in the snapping of his eyes, in the rigid line of his jaw.

"Jamie," she stammered, "go put on something dry."

Jamie, always sensitive to mood, cast an anxious glance back and forth, then silently complied.

"What is it?" she asked, and went forward and touched his arm.

He shook her hand away, and she backed away from him, stunned.

"You told me he was looking for a hero, someone to look up to. You never, ever mentioned the word daddy." His voice was very low, to keep Jamie from overhearing, but that in no way disguised the anger.

She felt the shock of it. She didn't know how to respond, but then he didn't seem to think a response was necessary.

"If you would have just told me, this never would have happened," he said.

"What happened?"

"He thinks Santa sent me to be his dad. Did you know he was going to think that?"

"I tried to tell you."

"Yeah, but not the whole truth."

"I thought I could look after it."

"You just think you can look after everything, don't you?"

She was beginning to feel her own temper flare. "As a matter of fact, I do. Because that's my reality. I look after everything, and I'm damn good at it, too."

"Oh, yeah? What about your broken stair? And how come you look sick every time the mail comes?"

She felt herself go very still. Jamie had told him she was not coping. But she was coping.

"I'm doing the best I can," she said, bravely. She felt like she was going to spoil it all by starting to cry.

Penny would have never cried in a situation like this. Never!

"Maybe I could have protected him, if you'd just told me."

"How? Stopped the snow from falling?"

"I could have left," he said.

"And walked home?"

"If I had to."

She studied him. He was not a good liar. And suddenly she knew the truth. "You could have left at anytime, couldn't you? You're not really snowed in here, at all."

It was his turn to look away. Penny would have been mighty pleased by that!

"Are you snowed in here?" she demanded.

"Not exactly. My truck went off the road. I could have winched it out, if I wanted to badly enough."

"How come you didn't?" And somehow she knew the answer was not going to be about the joy of her company.

"I wasn't convinced you could handle it up here."

"So, you lied to me."

"I omitted some of the facts."

Her new beginning was a complete farce. He had seen through her right away. He had seen that she was not strong and independent at all.

He had seen who she really was.

Weak. A failure. A woman who couldn't fix a step, and who worried about bills. A woman who couldn't even be trusted to have a Christmas vacation by herself.

"Well, that's all I did, too," she said, stiffly. "I omitted some of the facts. It was none of your business what was in his letter to Santa." To tell the truth, it was none of hers, either, and she rued the day she had decided it was. Not that she was telling Riley Keenan that. She had been quite vulnerable enough to him.

Funny, she had decided to try to be more like Penny.

But he had seen Beth anyway. And he had seemed to like that just fine last night.

In the end, he was just like Sam. He wanted to steal a few kisses, but he didn't want responsibility, commitment.

Though, to his credit, he was the one who had called off the kissing session last night.

Aha! He had probably been looking for an excuse ever since then to get away from her. That weak part of her wanted to beg him to rethink it, to stay, to return to the place of trust and closeness they had been at last night.

But that's not how Penny would handle a situation like this.

"You can leave now," she said, folding her arms over her chest.

"That would probably be the wisest thing," he agreed.

"Leave?" Jamie was standing in the doorway, looking from one to the other. His eyes filled with tears. "You're not going to leave, are you, Riley?"

"I think it might be better."

"But I'm going to be your little boy. You said I was at a good stage. No more stinky pants."

Riley sent her a black look, then got down on one knee. "Come here, tiger."

Jamie flew to him and threw his arms around

him. She saw that Riley gathered him close and held him hard.

"I'm not the man you think I am, Jamie. Santa didn't send me."

"Are you sure?"

Beth had to look away, because Riley looked like he was struggling with tremendous emotion.

After a long time, he said huskily. "I'm sure. You know what else I'm sure about? I will always be your friend."

Jamie looked unimpressed.

"Even if Riley is not the daddy you asked for, it still snowed," Beth reminded Jamie gently.

He let go of Riley and stood staring at her. "How did you know?" he finally asked. "How did you know I asked for a daddy? That I wanted snow?"

She said nothing, aghast at this slip, aghast that she knew his deepest secrets and he didn't want her to.

"You read my letter to Santa, didn't you?"

"Jamie—"

He gave her a look of angry bewildered hurt, and then he turned and ran from them both, ran into his room and shut the door.

"Beth." Riley took a step toward her. He looked like he was going to touch her. "I'm sorry."

She flinched away from his touch and his hand fell to his side.

"I really am sorry," he said.

The last thing she wanted from him was his pity.

She turned away from him. "It's not your fault," she said. "Just go."

Silence. She could feel his presence for a long time, and then it was gone.

She took several deep, steadying breaths. She must not cry. Not now.

She had done that very well. She had not begged to be loved. She had been strong. She had been a woman her sister would be proud of.

Now was not the time to suddenly remember that for all that her sister had been outgoing and adventurous, in the end they had all paid too high a price for that.

And yes, Penny had been independent, but she had also been alone, except for her sister and her son. Penny had been unable to compromise at all. Unable to lean on others.

Now was not the time to realize that the real Bethany was not only weak, and a failure, but she wanted to be with someone. She did not want to be alone.

No, now was not the time to think of that at all.

She went and knocked on Jamie's door.

"Go away."

She turned the handle, but felt his small weight hurdle against the door.

"I'm wrapping presents," he yelled, and furiously crinkled paper to prove it.

How could he be wrapping presents? She had packed all the bags and boxes. She knew what they had brought and what they hadn't.

She had bought herself a present from him, a sweater, that she had planned for them to wrap together tonight.

But come to think of it, she hated that sweater.

It was bland and boring, a librarian's sweater. Suddenly it represented everything she had tried so hard not to be. And she had not fooled anybody for one second.

She went to the window. She could see Riley walking in the distance, kicking up snow. His clothes had been wet when he left. What if he got sick and died?

Penny probably would have said, *I hope he does get sick and die.*

Beth tried to say it, but the words got all clogged up in her throat, and she was totally confused about who she was.

She could hear Jamie still crinkling paper.

She went and turned off the stove. No one wanted soup, it appeared.

So, this was the Christmas she was going to give her nephew. He was going to lock himself in his bedroom, she was going to eat soup by herself, and when she was done doing that she was going to cry.

On second thought, she could pass on the soup.

She threw herself down on the couch. She'd just

get straight to the crying part. But the truth was, she felt so exhausted, too exhausted even to cry. A weight, dark and heavy was pressing down on her. She would just shut her eyes for a few minutes. Until Jamie came out of his bedroom.

And then she would read him stories, and cuddle with him, and try to make things the way they used to be before she had made the mistake of coming here.

She could be his whole world again. She would learn how to fix the steps. That shouldn't be such a big deal.

Her eyes closed. She breathed in the heavenly scent of the Christmas tree and she slept.

She awoke, feeling very cold.

She sat up on the couch, thinking, "I've let the fire go out." Riley had been gone only a short time, and already she was not doing well. She had to show him she could be competent. She had to show herself!

But when she got up off the couch, she noticed the chill was sliding in the front cabin door that was open six or seven inches.

For a moment, she didn't comprehend.

And then she saw the door where Jamie had cordoned himself off in the bedroom was now wide-open.

She raced to it. There was Christmas wrapping paper shredded all over the floor.

But there was no Jamie.

And no Buddy Bear.

She raced to the front door.

A small set of footprints followed the larger ones down the snow-covered road.

Chapter 10

Looking at those small, forlorn prints in the snow, Beth felt panic rising. She scanned the horizon, but she saw no sign of a small boy. How long had he been gone? Half an hour? Or more?

She cried out his name, but the great white all around her made her voice seem small and insignificant. Only chilling silence answered her. Helpless terror threatened to engulf her, but she forced herself to take a deep, calming breath.

Panic would not help Jamie.

She needed to be calm and strong, right now, to think with absolute clarity. She needed to go after him, but this country was unforgiving. If she did not think out each step, carefully and concisely, disaster could be the result.

She knew that Penny would have just gone running out after him, with no thought, shoving on any shoes, putting on the first jacket that came under her hand. And she knew that Penny would have been wrong.

Deliberately, but swiftly, Beth chose dry clothes and boots. She shoved a candy bar in her pocket, and took the first-aid kit that hung by the door.

She tried to figure out what Jamie was wearing. The snowsuit was gone from beside the fire and so were his boots.

But both items must have been slightly damp. Why hadn't she asked Riley more about hypothermia when she had the chance?

She realized, just as panic would not help Jamie, neither would recriminations. They would just cloud her thinking.

It occurred to her that maybe all her life recriminations had been clouding her thinking, preventing her from seeing the truth about herself. She had always had a tendency to focus on what she did wrong, instead of what she did right.

One thing that she had always done right—she had always put Jamie first in her life. She had always let love guide her where he was concerned.

And she would let it guide her now.

She stepped out into the swirling storm. Had the

snow thickened since they had gone sledding? Almost certainly. It was already swallowing some of Jamie's tracks. Had it done the same to the tracks he was following?

Again, she bit back panic, and forced herself to survey the situation calmly. It was very obvious where the road was; a wide swatch of white cut through the trees, and he would have had no reason to wander from it.

Assuming he was going after Riley.

What if he was just running away? Furious with her for her betrayal, heart broken that his daddy plans were not working out.

The panic tried to rise again, but again she stopped it. She knew it would not serve her. She needed to think clearly, she needed all her strength. Panic would steal those qualities from her.

She chose to trust love and believe in courage. Her own. Just like that, she took a deep, deep breath, and chose.

Walking along, she had a sudden sense of knowing, finally, exactly who she was.

And what she was prepared to fight for.

The truck, when Riley finally got to it, was buried under snow. It had been a hell of a job getting here. He should have thought to take the snowshoes out of the rafters of the cabin, but in his great haste to leave he had not thought it through clearly. Instead he had ended up plowing through the deepening snow on foot.

It was exhausting work—not that it was a bad thing to be exhausted. He had learned, over the years, physical exhaustion was as good a remedy as any for a mind that wanted to obsessively dwell on things best left alone.

Riley wiped some of the snow off the side truck window with his sleeve, then reached into the box and uncovered a shovel.

It felt good to have this task to do, to turn off his mind, to not think of the pain he had left behind him.

He should have followed his first desire, the one that had put his self-preservation first. He should have never looked for all those flimsy excuses to go back to the cabin. He should have left the Cavells alone. He had always known he had the capacity to ruin their Christmas.

What were they doing right now? Had Beth managed to get Jamie out of the bedroom? Little kids were resilient, weren't they? He'd probably forgotten all about it by now. He and Beth were probably sitting on the couch, reading a story, making their last-minute preparations for Christmas.

They were probably—

The thought stopped, abruptly, and his every sense went on red alert. He listened. What had he heard? The wind in the treetops? The creak of ice freezing on water? He listened longer, but heard nothing.

He went back to work with the shovel, but the hair on the back of his neck rose. The feeling was eerily familiar, exactly like before, when he had tried to drive by that small flicker of light on Christmas Eve six years ago.

It was Christmas Eve, again.

He stood motionless in the falling snow, straining to hear, and even though he heard nothing, he tossed down the shovel. He took the bank up to the road in three giant leaps, and stood there, chest heaving, every sense crackling with alertness.

Nothing. He began to run down the road, desperately plowing the deep snow. After a few minutes his legs felt as though he was pushing through wet sand, and his breath came hard, but he ran on, his eyes scanning, searching, his ears listening so hard they ached.

The road twisted, and he flew around the bend, and saw what looked to be a little pile of rags in the middle of the road.

His lungs screamed and his legs burned, and he ignored both, poured on what little energy he had left, slid to his knees at the little bundle of boy, curled up in a ball.

"Jamie," he whispered, "it's okay. I'm here."

The bundle was quivering, shaking uncontrollably.

He slipped his hands under and lifted Jamie gently, held him tight against his chest, and rocked. He scanned the tear-streaked face, and felt relief. The quivering was not the first signs of hypothermia setting in, thank God.

It was from Jamie crying.

"I...I...I lost Buddy Bear," he whimpered. "I was following your footsteps, and the snow was too heavy and way too deep. Sometimes I couldn't find your tracks anymore, and I kept falling down, and last time I got up I noticed I didn't have Buddy Bear, and I didn't know where I lost him and now I don't know where he is."

Riley wrapped his arms tighter, and held the boy hard against him. Jamie's hot tears splashed down the opening in his jacket, reached his skin.

"Shh. We'll find him. I promise."

He felt the tension ease from the small boy's body, and he wiped his sleeve over the tear-stained face.

"I was so s-s-scared," Jamie sobbed. "I've never been so scared." He tucked his head against Riley's shoulder and wept.

A terrible thought occurred to Riley. Why had the child been following his footsteps? Had something happened to Beth? Had Jamie come in search of him?

"Where's your aunt?"

"She's sleeping," Jamie said. "I tiptoed by her on the couch."

"What? Why?" What if Beth was awake by now? Undoubtably she'd be awake by now. She'd be scared witless.

"I wanted to give you a Christmas present," Jamie said in a small voice.

Riley rose to his feet, the child cradled against his chest, and began to jog toward the cabin. He ran faster, thinking of her pain, thinking he could not allow her to be in pain.

"You shouldn't have done that," he said, firmly. "You hear me? You shouldn't have come out here without telling your aunt. You might have gotten yourself into really serious trouble."

"I know," Jamie said.

"If you ever do something so dumb again, I'm going to tan your hide."

Riley wanted to only hold the child, only love him. But sometimes love meant being firm, setting the boundaries that were not to be crossed, ever. It was what he had to do. It was what a father would do.

Draw the lines strongly when the mistake was such a huge one, when the situation had such devastating potential to be life-threatening.

If Jamie had wandered off the road, and into the woods in this storm, how would they have found him? Riley's heart beat painfully in his chest thinking about it.

"I had to give you your Christmas present," Jamie said. "I had to."

"Nothing," he said, his breath coming in ragged gasps, "is worth risking your life for. Do you understand? You ever do something like that to Beth, or me, again, and I'll tan your hide."

He noticed, abstractly, he seemed to be planning a future for the boy that he was a participant in.

"I'm not sure what that means, tan your hide," Jamie said, and snuggled deeper against him, wiped his nose on the front of Riley's coat.

"It means a spanking."

"Spanking," Jamie whispered. "That means very bad boy. I guess Santa's not going to come, after all."

"Santa must know a thing or two about forgiveness. He's been in the joy and happiness business for a long time. There would be nobody to give presents to, if only the perfect people got them."

Forgiveness. The word tickled at the back of his mind, but then Riley saw something on the road up ahead of him, a colorful small heap, not big enough to be a person. He arrived at it and stopped.

Jamie peeped down. "That's him," he said.

It was a clumsily wrapped Christmas parcel. When he stooped and picked it up, Buddy Bear's little glass eye looked up at him through the torn, soggy paper.

He thrust the package into Jamie's arms.

Jamie whispered to the bear that he was sorry he'd dropped him. He tucked him close, and then put his thumb in his mouth. Riley had never seen him suck his thumb before. It reminded him how very small he was, despite his nearly adult capacity to carry on a conversation.

He pushed himself to keep moving fast. He felt Jamie sigh against him, as he curled his body around the partially wrapped teddy bear.

Riley's lungs felt like they were going to burst, and his legs muscles burned as though they were on fire. He knew he was going to have to slow down, soon. He couldn't keep up this pace.

And yet, when he thought of what she must be feeling, he could not make himself go slower. And then he caught a glimpse of her jacket, through the trees, where the road twisted above him.

"Beth," he yelled. "Beth!"

She halted and looked down through the trees, then shouted, "Have you got him? Riley, is Jamie with you?"

"He's okay. I've got him."

She leaped off the road, and was running down through the trees toward them, tripping and slipping and sliding.

Silly, when he was so tired, to go off the road,

too, to start running up that hill toward her, but he did.

She slid to a stop in front of him. She was covered with snow from practically tumbling down that hill, and gasping for breath.

He saw it in her eyes. Immediately and without question. The thing he felt completely unworthy of.

But just in case he didn't get it, she stood on her tiptoes and kissed Riley right on the mouth. Passionately, holding nothing back. So that there was absolutely no question what she felt.

What was left of his defenses crumpled.

And then she held out her arms, and he put Jamie in them, and she buried her face in the black silk of his hair and then kissed him all over.

"What on earth were you thinking?" she asked the child, furiously, when she was done smothering him with kisses. She set him on the ground and put her hands on her hips. "Well? What?"

"I had to give Riley his Christmas present. I had to."

Riley thought the spanking lecture had not been nearly as effective as he had thought it was being at the time. Maybe he shouldn't have proffered Santa's forgiveness quite so quickly. What did he know about Santa, after all?

"But you don't have anything to give Riley—" she stopped. Her eyes fell on the package. And then she started to cry.

Riley took her in his arms, gathered her tight, caught her teardrops with his glove. "It's okay," he said, over and over. "It's okay."

Jamie became impatient, and inserted his solid little body between them. But rather than separating them, it became a circle.

Squished between them, and obviously damned happy about it, Jamie managed to shove the soggy parcel up to Riley. "Here. You can open it now. The wrapping was better, before it got wet."

Riley had already glimpsed the contents of that package. He did not want to take it, and yet as Jamie held it out to him, he had a sensation of having no choice. He took the package, but as it passed from Jamie's hand to his, he felt a sudden and strange awareness.

It was a sensation of something of Jamie coming into him: the part of Jamie that believed in magic. And miracles. And Christmas.

Slowly he peeled the paper off. Buddy Bear's head emerged from the package, and glared at them with his beady eye.

For a moment Riley could not trust himself to speak.

Finally he said, choked, "I can't take your bear, Jamie."

"I don't have anything else to give you."

Yes, you do. And he'd already given it. Trust. Faith. Hope. Love.

"I can't take your bear," Riley said again, his voice hoarse.

"Yes, you can," Jamie said softly. "You need him way more than me. I can tell. You look really sad sometimes, Riley, and Buddy Bear is the best when you're sad. He listens so good."

Jamie, whom Riley had abandoned back there at the cabin only an hour or two ago, had already put that betrayal aside. Put it aside and dipped into the spring of his young spirit, turned around and given him back everything he had in the whole world.

Suddenly Riley felt a wave of shame. He had tried to make Beth believe, somehow, it was her fault he was going, that he was abandoning them at the Christmas cabin. And he saw now that that was not true.

The truth was he was afraid of the love shining like a beacon from Beth's big green eyes. Afraid he would be unworthy of the grave honor Jamie was holding out to him.

Last night, Riley had known the truth, briefly. *Forgiveness.* The word tickled his brain again, a piece of the puzzle looking for its place.

And then Riley knew the truth. He could not get on with his life until he forgave himself for his failure six years ago.

That's what had driven him away from the warmth of that cabin. It was not that he did not want to be a daddy.

It was that he wanted it so much. Just like running down the hallway of that burning trailer, it felt like he wanted it more than life itself. It felt as if failure was not an option.

Because he had failed, he realized he had developed a survival mechanism. The more strongly he felt anything over the last years, the harder he had run from it.

And then, despite all his efforts, here he was, being given a second chance. Even though he had not asked for it. Even though he did not deserve it.

He understood, suddenly, clearly, that he was in the presence of Love. That he had been forgiven by something much larger than himself, and to hold on to his failures and transgressions in the face of that would be wrong.

Forgiveness was not a word. It was a feeling. And he felt it, deeply and genuinely. It was over. What had happened six years ago was over. He had been given a slate as clean as if he had been born yesterday.

A long, long time ago, a child had come to give a gift to the world, too.

The world twisted the message, and forgot it, and misinterpreted it, and yet the message remained, pure and undiluted in the incredible innocence that was the heart of a child, a child like Jamie. So His message could never be totally turned away from, or totally forgotten, or totally misused.

Riley realized he had a gift to give, too.

And it was not giving Beth and Jamie the cabin for free.

More was being asked of him. Much, much more. He had known it all along, perhaps even from the first moment that he had seen her at the airport. He had been attracted to the wonderful adventure he was being asked to say yes to, and wanted to run at the very same time.

He had known last night.

And maybe that's why he had been so eager to find an excuse to run this morning.

He had never before given the gift he was being asked to give now.

He was being asked to give his heart. He knew it to be battered and bruised, and that it would be no bargain for the person on the receiving end.

He was being asked to give his imperfections.

All of himself, good and bad, strong and weak, sometimes close to perfect and sometimes terribly flawed.

He had known last night that she would accept him just as he was. He had known Love had found him. He had known and rejoiced and been terrified at the same time.

He tucked the bear safe inside his jacket, and put the small boy on his shoulders.

He wrapped his arm around Beth's waist and kissed her on the mouth, long and hard. He felt the tenderness of her response. And her answer to the question he had yet to ask.

"What you think?" he asked her. "Have we wandered long enough, Bethany? Is it time to go on home?"

She was looking at him, her eyes shining with welcome, with warmth, with tenderness, with discovery.

"Yes," she said, "it's time to find our way home."

Epilogue

Home.

It shone out of the darkness ahead of him, golden light splashing across snow. Riley walked toward it, his breath forming icy clouds around him.

No snowstorm this year, and colder than it had been last year. Much colder. The stars winked in the inky-black sky above him.

They had debated going to the cabin, but in the end they had decided to stay home to celebrate Christmas. His mother was getting a little too old for roughing it, not that she would ever admit it.

Besides, the truth was he hadn't been able to figure out how to get the pony up there without Jamie figuring it out.

He and Beth had read the letter together this year, giggling like school kids. She and Jamie had moved from Arizona to Bragg Creek early in the year, and at her insistence, gotten their own place.

Riley had courted her with all the fervor of a callow boy. He had brought her flowers and wined and dined her and fallen so crazy in love with her that most days he didn't know the difference between up and down.

He thought marrying her would put him out of his misery, but he was, truth be told, more crazy in love than ever. Being around her made him feel like he'd been drinking fine wine, intoxicated, heady on the nectar of life.

"Dear Santa," she had read over his shoulder, her lemon scent tickling his nose. "How are you? Is everything good at the North Pole? How are the reindeers and elfs?

"I have been a very good boy this year. I would like a pony for Christmas, or a puppy. The Mc-Caffreys have some black labs if you don't know where to get one."

She wrapped her arms around his shoulders and squeezed.

"Are you crying?" he asked.

"He wants normal things, Riley," she breathed. "Of course I'm crying."

But, the truth was, she cried all the time right now. She cried when his mother knitted little tiny booties, and she cried when they shopped for the bassinet. She cried the night they whispered in bed that if it was a boy they would call him Ben.

"I'm happy," she told him, when he worried about all the tears. "I'm just so happy."

He thought that was a damned funny way to show it, but he was learning women were deeper, and more mysterious than he had ever figured. It was going to take him a whole lifetime to figure her out. Or maybe longer. Thank God.

"P.S.," Riley had finished reading the letter, "Thank you for bringing me a daddy last year. My dad is the best dad in the whole world. He is just what Auntie Mommy needed. And me, too."

It had been Riley's turn to feel a little choked.

He had learned something every single day since he had been a part of this circle of love. But the most important thing he had learned was this: being a hero was not about jumping into blazing buildings, after all. He had felt, and would always feel, that in that situation he had no choice.

No, being a hero involved making tough choices. Scary choices. It meant choosing with the heart instead of the head, going with the gut instead of the mind.

Being a hero meant having the courage to let go of control and say yes to the incredible adventure of love.

Being a hero meant getting up at five in the

morning to go lace up Jamie's skates and put on his hockey pads in an ice-cold arena.

It meant holding a damp cloth on the back of Beth's neck when she was losing her cookies after eating the oysters he'd gone all the way to Calgary to get for her.

The little black pony with the red ribbon around his neck nickered softly behind him as they shuffled through the snow and the darkness toward the lights of home.

"Yeah, yeah," Riley said. "I know. Being a true hero means being all grown up and believing in Santa Claus." Well, if not in Santa Claus, precisely, at least in the spirit of Santa Claus.

A spirit of giving and selflessness, a spirit that made a man more than he had ever believed he could be. It was the only spirit that could really change the world, a spirit of love.

A spirit that began with a child in a stable on a cold starry night not very different than this one.

* * * * *

REQUEST YOUR FREE BOOKS!

2 FREE NOVELS
FROM THE ROMANCE COLLECTION
PLUS 2 FREE GIFTS!

YES! Please send me 2 FREE novels from the Romance Collection and my 2 FREE gifts (gifts are worth about $10). After receiving them, if I don't wish to receive any more books, I can return the shipping statement marked "cancel." If I don't cancel, I will receive 4 brand-new novels every month and be billed just $5.99 per book in the U.S. or $6.49 per book in Canada. That's a saving of at least 25% off the cover price. It's quite a bargain! Shipping and handling is just 50¢ per book in the U.S. and 75¢ per book in Canada.* I understand that accepting the 2 free books and gifts places me under no obligation to buy anything. I can always return a shipment and cancel at any time. Even if I never buy another book, the two free books and gifts are mine to keep forever.

194/394 MDN FELQ

Name	(PLEASE PRINT)

Address	Apt. #

City	State/Prov.	Zip/Postal Code

Signature (if under 18, a parent or guardian must sign)

Mail to the **Reader Service:**
IN U.S.A.: P.O. Box 1867, Buffalo, NY 14240-1867
IN CANADA: P.O. Box 609, Fort Erie, Ontario L2A 5X3

Not valid for current subscribers to the Romance Collection
or the Romance/Suspense Collection.

Want to try two free books from another line?
Call 1-800-873-8635 or visit www.ReaderService.com.

* Terms and prices subject to change without notice. Prices do not include applicable taxes. Sales tax applicable in N.Y. Canadian residents will be charged applicable taxes. Offer not valid in Quebec. This offer is limited to one order per household. All orders subject to credit approval. Credit or debit balances in a customer's account(s) may be offset by any other outstanding balance owed by or to the customer. Please allow 4 to 6 weeks for delivery. Offer available while quantities last.

Your Privacy—The Reader Service is committed to protecting your privacy. Our Privacy Policy is available online at www.ReaderService.com or upon request from the Reader Service.

We make a portion of our mailing list available to reputable third parties that offer products we believe may interest you. If you prefer that we not exchange your name with third parties, or if you wish to clarify or modify your communication preferences, please visit us at www.ReaderService.com/consumerschoice or write to us at Reader Service Preference Service, P.O. Box 9062, Buffalo, NY 14269. Include your complete name and address.

ROM11

FAMOUS FAMILIES

YES! Please send me the *Famous Families* collection featuring the Fortunes, the Bravos, the McCabes and the Cavanaughs. This collection will begin with 3 FREE BOOKS and 2 FREE GIFTS in my very first shipment— and more valuable free gifts will follow! My books will arrive in 8 monthly shipments until I have the entire 51-book *Famous Families* collection. I will receive 2-3 free books in each shipment and I will pay just $4.49 U.S./$5.39 CDN for each of the other 4 books in each shipment, plus $2.99 for shipping and handling.* If I decide to keep the entire collection, I'll only have paid for 32 books because 19 books are free. I understand that accepting the 3 free books and gifts places me under no obligation to buy anything. I can always return a shipment and cancel at any time. My free books and gifts are mine to keep no matter what I decide.

268 HCN 0387   468 HCN 0387

Name _____ (PLEASE PRINT)

Address _____ Apt. #

City _____ State/Prov. _____ Zip/Postal Code

Signature (if under 18, a parent or guardian must sign)

Mail to the **Reader Service**:

IN U.S.A.: P.O. Box 1867, Buffalo, NY 14240-1867
IN CANADA: P.O. Box 609, Fort Erie, Ontario L2A 5X3

* Terms and prices subject to change without notice. Prices do not include applicable taxes. Sales tax applicable in N.Y. Canadian residents will be charged applicable taxes. This offer is limited to one order per household. All orders subject to approval. Credit or debit balances in a customer's account(s) may be offset by any other outstanding balance owed by or to the customer. Please allow 4 to 6 weeks for delivery. Offer available while quantities last. Offer not available to Quebec residents.

Your Privacy— The Reader Service is committed to protecting your privacy. Our Privacy Policy is available online at www.ReaderService.com or upon request from the Reader Service.

We make a portion of our mailing list available to reputable third parties that offer products we believe may interest you. If you prefer that we not exchange your name with third parties, or if you wish to clarify or modify your communication preferences, please visit us at www.ReaderService.com/consumerschoice or write to us at Reader Service Preference Service, P.O. Box 9062, Buffalo, NY 14269. Include your complete name and address.

FFBPA12